The wise bird Hoopoe

Alisher Nava'i

THE LANGUAGE
OF THE BIRDS

AuthorHouse™
1663 Liberty Drive, Suite 200
Bloomington, IN 47403
www.authorhouse.com
Phone: 1-800-839-8640

AuthorHouse™ UK Ltd.
500 Avebury Boulevard
Central Milton Keynes, MK9 2BE
www.authorhouse.co.uk
Phone: 08001974150

First published by AuthorHouse 9/29/2006

ISBN: 1-4259-1248-6 (sc)

Library of Congress Control Number: 2006900434

Printed in the United States of America
Bloomington, Indiana

This book is printed on acid-free paper.

Director of OOO «Doys»: Babajanov Dilmurod
Chief Editor: Shavkat Azimov

INTRODUCTION

"Know all humankind: Amity with the world is the great blessing,
Enmity the greatest curse."

Alisher Nava'i

The Great Silk Road is known for its poets. One of the most important of these is Alisher Nava'i. His numerous writings, endowments, and his life example have had lasting influence. Today, in the modern country of Uzbekistan, he is revered above all other poets. The name of Alisher Nava'i is visible throughout the country. Major streets, theatres, museums, parks, and even a province and city are named after him. His proverbs are on the tongues of Uzbeks, Turkmen and Tajiks. He is considered the father of the Uzbek language and one of the greatest poets of Central Asia. He wrote for peace and he spoke against oppression.

Nava'i lived from 1441 to 1501 in Herat, Afghanistan. As a child, his skill for poetry was recognized and his father made sure he received the proper training. When his foster brother Husain Baykara became the Emir, Nava'i naturally became the second most powerful person. He was a wise statesman, who advised Baykara on many matters. Once when Baykara's son's rebelled as a prince of nearby Balkh, Nava'i paid a personal visit to persuade him otherwise. Nava'i was a good steward of his high position and helped establish many needed institutions. "Nawai (Nava'i) is reputed to have founded, restored and endowed no fewer than 370 mosques, schools, libraries, hospitals and other pious and charitable institutions in Khurasan alone,"[1]

Nava'i's greatest contribution, however, comes in the realm of the arts. Under his guidance and patronage of art and culture Herat blossomed to one of its finest periods. Nava'i himself wrote over 10,000 lines of poetry, including at least stx epic poems. While he was still alive, his contemporaries considered him to be the best Eastern Turkish writer ever. This claim is still true today. "The impact of Navai's works on all Turkic peoples and languages cannot be overestimated. He exerted a profound influence not only on later Central Asian authors who wrote in Caghatay up till the beginning of the 20th century, but also on the development of Azeri,

---

[1] Devereux, Robert. *Muslim World* 54 1964, p 270 –287.

Turkmen, Uyghur, Tatar and Ottoman Turkish literatures."[2]

The life and works of Nava'i are also relevant for today's politically and spiritually rigid world. He was a Sufi who blurred the lines of what was right and wrong. Sometimes his writings imitated other popular works but with his own twist. Written around 1499, "The Language of the Birds" ("Lison-ut Tayr") is one such writing. It is based on Farid ud-din Attar's twelfth century "The Conference of the Birds" which Nava'i read and adored as a child. Nava'i is a masterful adapter who worked at inspiring his fellow Turkish people.

"The Language of the Birds" is a story about the hard journey to Sufi enlightenment. In it we are shown that a guide is very important for the road. This is the role the Shaikhs play in Sufism. Anyone serious about finding enlightenment must have a discipler that will point him the way. The actual steps, however, the disciples must take themselves. In the book the wise bird Hoopoe become the birds' Shaikh. As he listens to each bird's excuse he admonishes each one with the exact anecdotes that they need to hear. These stories that Hoopoe uses so capably often come from the oral history of the Silk Road and Islam. Suffering and difficulty are the norm, while easy and relaxed lives are shown as superficial. When these birds do make it all the way to God, everyone including the reader is surprised at what they find.

Our preliminary translation and publication of "The Language of the Birds" is Alisher Nava'i's premiere for the English world. It is our hope that a Nava'i series will follow and that the Western world's understanding of Central Asia and interest in this beautiful land will grow. Central Asia is about culture and history, warm hospitality and a poet living and writing thoughtfully about peace, tolerance and acceptance of others. We also hope that this book will advance your spiritual pilgrimage to God and his flower garden of truth.

---

[2] Subtelny, M.E. *Islamic Encyclopedia*

PREFACE

A Note on the Translation and Important Literary Terms

When the terms or meanings were unclear, they were discussed with Uzbek experts, and sometimes checked with the original Chaghatay (old Uzbek). The text used was Sharafiddin Sharipov's 1991 prose translation, which was part of the Uzbek Literature's Flower Garden series. We have included most of his annotation. However, we did not include the prelude and epilogue, as it is quite separate from the original story. For those wanting to compare with the Uzbek version the story begins in chapter fourteen.

Generally, proper nouns were transliterated based on the new Latin Uzbek alphabet. Commonly known proper nouns were translated into their English equivalents. For example, Yusef of the Old Testament was translated as Joseph. Also, when it was judged that Nava'i himself was speaking into the story double quotation marks were used ("). Sometimes, however, Nava'i does speak through Hoopoe the wise bird, and as with the original, the speaker is not always marked in our text.

The Turkish and Persian writings of the Middle Ages obtained a high quality of flowery descriptions, metaphors, and paradoxes. The following sentence from "The Language of the Birds" is a wonderful example of the Turkish and Persian style:

> His home is so beautiful that my tongue's pencil is insufficient to edit the few thoughts that I do manage to speak correctly. All right, since the bird's dream of what they have heard, let me say one or two words about the shah's characteristics. If I describe one thousandth of them, then evidently I was able to describe him from one till only a thousand.

The first sentence is obviously a contradiction as rationally there is no need to edit something if it is done correctly, however, there is beauty for the mind that can see beyond what makes sense. Also, the use metaphors such as, the tongue as a pencil, is very typical when it comes to describing people. The next two

sentences are a play with numbers in a roundabout fashion; this is also typical of the highly educated poets of the time. Nava'i writes that a description of 1/1000th of the shah's characteristics equals 1000; mathematically this means that the shah has one million characteristics in total. It is our hope that the reader will be able to savor the style and forms of this foreign book.

While translating this book we made some changes in the English for the story to make sense to the average reader. We have sought to make this Middle Ages story come alive in the English language in its own unique way. The native English person with some interest in Central Asian literature was our target culture. However, the foreignism of this ancient text is still there to make the reader think in new ways. "We need the ancients precisely to the degree they are dissimilar to us, and translation should emphasize their exotic, distant character, making it intelligible as such".[1] We need unaccustomed foreign literature to make us think in fresh ways.

There are many ways of translating, and many ways that Nava'i's meanings can be translated. For every what that we have translated, we have our why. We hope that any changes that we have made are improvements that will help Nava'i's thoughts connect with today's English reader.

---

[1] Jose Ortega Y Gasset, 'The Misery and the Splendor of Translation' in Lawrence Venuti, ed., *The Translation Studies Reader*, London, Routledge, 2000, p. 62.

Let me learn by paradox
    that the way down is the way up,
    that to be low is to be high,
    that the broken heart is the healed heart,
    that the contrite spirit is the rejoicing spirit,
    that the repenting soul is the victorious soul,
    that to have nothing is to possess all,
    that to bear the cross is to wear the crown,
    that to give is to receive,
    that the valley is the place of vision.
Lord, in the daytime stars can be seen from deepest wells,
    and the deeper the wells the brighter thy stars shine;
Let me find thy light in my darkness,
        thy life in my death,
        thy joy in my sorrow,
        thy grace in my sin,
        thy riches in my poverty,
        thy glory in my valley.

                – from The Valley of Vision: A Collection of
                Puritan Prayers and Devotions

THE LANGUAGE OF THE BIRDS

I

The Birds Assemble, Quarrel Over the Seat of Honor[1] and Realize They need a Ruler

One day the birds of the garden, sea and wilderness gathered into their choruses for a meeting. They composed a lovely song. After their feast they wanted to go up to the sky.

However, none of them had their designated place for the meeting. There was no seating order and so a speckled crow sat in front of a parrot, and a bedraggled crow sat at a higher position than a nightingale and a dove. A vulture sat in the seat of honor instead of a falcon. A Carrion vulture snubbed a peacock and sat in front of it. Menial birds took the seats of adept ones. Birds with no crowns occupied the honored places and birds with crowns sat by the door.

The birds by the door began quarrelling, but the birds in honored places did not listen. Consequently, there was uproar. After quarrelling for a long time the birds began discussing the crisis. As time passed the crisis increased.

They realized that they needed a shah who was honest and conscientious. One who could establish order and justice, so that people in lower and upper classes would not be harmed in the shade of his kingdom. Thereby they hoped that others would not mistreat the people of higher class. Everybody wanted a pure and wise shah. However, there was no fair shah among

---

[1] The tradition of the 'seat of honor' is still common in Central Asia. The most honored guests are to sit by the corner of the tablecloth that is farthest away from the door.

them. Therefore, they were sorrowful, desperate, and in pitiful shape. Their tunes were mournful, as the crisis weighed heavy on their hearts. They began to suffer like half slaughtered birds.

II

The Birds are Shocked When They Cannot Find a Shah for Themselves and Hoopoe Tells Them about Semurgh

Hoopoe is a bird that enjoys the wise light. His lineage is glorious and extremely elevated. He is decorated with the crown of one who shows the right way. He flies in God's throne room and like Gabriel all kinds of secrets are obvious to him.

He intended to sing of his candle and entered the meeting when it was about to burn up like a moth. 'O oblivious flock!' he said. 'Your situation is mixed with ignorance. There is an incomparable shah in the world. A thousand tongues are inadequate to describe him. He is the king of all birds. He is always aware of your state. He is near you, but you are far from him. He is able to meet you, but you remain separated from him. His every feather is radiant with thousands of colors, and every color has a thousand attractive patterns. People are not able to comprehend his designs and colors. His intelligence is victorious and there is no way of doing what he does.

'He lives on a mountain called Qof[2] and there is known as Anqo[3] there. His name, Semurgh[4] has found fame all over the world. At the archway of the supreme sky his kind is filled with perfection. In terms of his origin there is nothing like him in the supreme sky.

'You are infinitely far from that shah, but he is closer to you than your neck veins. If anyone is far from him when he is alive then it is better to be dead!'

---

[2] Qof is a legendary mountain that saddles the world.
[3] Anqo is the legendary bird of Qof mountain.
[4] Literally means 'thirty birds' in Persian.

III

After Hoopoe Described Semurgh the Birds were Joyful and Asked More About Him

The birds were in a frenzy. All around Hoopoe they began shouting, 'Oh, your breath is life-giving and your speech is enchanting! Both are useful for the soul and heart. You have been accepted at Solomon's feast and you travel as his envoy. In his service you have become close to him. For his sake how many stopping places have you passed over? How many valleys have you flown over? You have made it to the final destination.

'Just like Gabriel was beside Mustafo[5] you have now been where Solomon has been. You accompanied him in good and bad times. When he enjoyed life you were his dear advisor. If he wanted to know how Bilqis[6] was doing you would immediately set off to the city where she lived. You soothed his heart by informing him about her.

'In this way you were a help to the Prophet. You accompanied him while he waited for his difficulties to show another side. If he had a feast either in the city or in the desert, we would all use our wings to form a parasol for him. Hundreds of thousands of birds served as a tent for him and you resided with him in this shade[7]. Thus at the feast he made you happy and aware of his secrets as a confidant.

'Truth[8] assigned you a high position. Therefore, every feather and member of you obtained significance. Deception, however, hinders us. For this reason make us aware of this shah's secrets. Tell us the stories of his qualities and show us the right way to be of his kind.

'You should save us from ignorance and banish naivety and lowliness. Tell us about his secrets and enjoy explaining it. Keep us from being consumed with anger and direct the search for our shah. If we reach our goal, we will be extremely grateful to you.'

---

[5] 'Selected' or 'chosen.' Here it implies Muhammad and one of his attributes.

[6] The Queen of Sabo (Sheba). In chapter 27 of the Qur'an the story goes that Hudhud (Hoopoe) had informed Solomon (who knew the language of the birds) of a glorious Queen from Sabo that worshipped the sun. With the assistance of Hudhud Solomon then proceeded to convert her and she became his beloved woman.

[7] Legend has it that, while the birds formed a parasol to protect Solomon from the hot sun, it was Hoopoe that he needed to find water for his ablutions.

[8] 'Truth' is another name for God.

IV

Hoopoe's Impressions after the Birds
asked about Semurgh

With his breath, Hoopoe scattered sugar and sweet words were produced. After having seen the birds in distress he answered them in this way,

'Let me tell you what I know about him and about his secrets that have entered my heart. However, to tell of the legend will not be enough. The people will not find his treasure with mere words. For what we want to do is a tremendous work. The shah and his palace are paramount, but the road is hard and the valleys long. Of course, you want me to speak about the shah but if I talked for a thousand years it would not be enough.

'No one can make sense of him, but his name must always be remembered. In order to do so one must first clean his mouth with the water of life ten times, maybe a hundred times, maybe limitless times. After having your tongue and mouth purified in this way, it is possible to cautiously mention his name.

'However, the shah is above these things to a high degree. His home is so beautiful that my tongue's pencil is insufficient to edit the few thoughts that I do manage to speak correctly. All right, since the bird's dream of what they have heard, let me say one or two words about the shah's characteristics. If I describe one thousandth of them, then evidently I was able to describe him from one till only a thousand.

'Our Shah is the shah of all shahs and he is always aware of our state. He is one, but he is also the owner of more than a thousand features. His features have spread all over the world and everything in the world has come from him. If he does not want anything to happen it will not happen. Nobody can even find a way to take a breath without his will. Whether you are great or low, or your stature and attributes are big or small, you are subject to him.

'In each of his wings he has thousands of feathers and they fill a great space all around him. All of the feathers have the deep knowledge of the sea. It cannot be determined whether he is complex or simple. Your life is in his song and that's why you fly everywhere. Get to know him like the blood that is part of your body and as the soul that is alive in your body.

He is dearer than the soul in your body; there is nothing closer than him.

'However, you are a thousand years apart from him, as it should be. Perhaps it is good that you are far from any possibility, for why should one have a soul if he is a long way from it! If the soul is without him what use is it! Whomever the shah blesses with union, he will still appear attractive from two worlds away. To live in separation from him, however, is more perilous than death. It is worse than being in eight paradises and then falling through seven hells.

'However, it is not easy to meet a shah like him. One cannot see him without enduring difficulties and great striving. Besides the thousand varieties of difficulties on the way, one needs genuine desire. The valley is extremely distant and on the way one can meet much misfortune. Hence, one should fly for a long way without stopping, yet the life of several Karkases[9] will not be enough to do this.

'There are many worrisome rivers, but perhaps it is more correct to call them bitter poison. The mountain blades have been stretched to the sky and are in position to mercilessly shed blood. Flames border the wastelands and can be seen in the sky everywhere. The forests are full of various adversities. Every branch consists of misery and every leaf contains misfortune. In the sky the heavens are struck and the floating clouds rain down stones. Sparks from the clouds put the world on fire. There is no place to stay for night. One cannot find water or grain to sustain their strength. It is unknown if thousands of birds doing the journey flying for a thousand years have persevered and reached their aim.

'However, anybody who gives his or her soul to this requirement realizes it is better than a hundred permanent lives. The various birds of the world's garden must fly and alight over and over again for many days, singing the tunes of a perishing garden and keeping on flying in the right direction. It is good if they sacrifice their lives for their beloved while in the valley of separation. This delightful death will be worth one hundred thousand souls and it will take the place of eternal life. If a bird is fortunate, and having both wealth and guidance passes over the limitless wasteland, undoubtedly, he will see that eternal garden. He will be eternally one with the shah and reach Truth's shadow. His position will be as high as God's throne and whoever's head his shadow falls upon will be blessed.'

---

[9] Long-living birds.

V

The Birds Ask Hoopoe about Semurgh's Origin and Hoopoe Tells Them a True Legend and of the Secretive Bird's Mark

All the birds enjoined,

'O guide, tell us how to start this work. If he is the sultan and all birds are his soldiers, and he is in people's midst, how will Semurgh be seen? Who has seen his position, character, name and kind? How can one visit the holy place? Report to us what is allowable and what is forbidden, because these things are difficult to discern. The clever are inadequate. One hundred wise men would become crazy in this effort.'

VI

A Description of a Chinese City when Semurgh's Fairy landed there

Hoopoe said the following to the birds:

'It happened in a city whose name meant 'Eastern China'. It was not a city as in its breadth it was becoming equal to the whole world. All races were situated in it. The city's appearance was better than the Garden of Eden and its water more enchanting than the rivulet of Paradise.

'One night the shah began to fly all over the world. Suddenly he landed in this Chinese city that was like paradise on earth. That night as he was flying over the city it became illuminated from top to bottom. The people who were aware of it were baffled. In the rustle of his flying, one feather fell out and magnificently decorated all of China. That feather was so colorful and elaborate that it is difficult to describe.

'The following day the nation changed back to its former state and people began staring at the feather's form and color. Vigorously everybody began drawing the feather's design and recomposing it in their imagination. Everybody started making illustrations and the whole nation was busy.

'Among them, a certain man's pictures reached a degree of perfection. His name was Moniy[10]. His pencil worked wonders and people who

---

[10] His full name is Moniy ibn Fatak. In Eastern legend he is famous for his traditional artwork.

saw his art were amazed. That's why people say that Moniy's studio is in China. Also, that feather is said to still be in celestial China. There is unbelievable beauty there and to an extent all beauty is based on the appearance of this feather.

'Nobody could say that they saw Semurgh. Not many words about him were said. Nobody could say anything about his origin, because not even someone with sharp eyes was able to see him. On that feather many feathers grew. They displayed his quality. On this feather appeared immeasurable designs. The colors were incomparable. Only experts knew how to name them.

'Although nobody can describe this bird, no one is actually without him. To follow his orders is all of our responsibility and obligation. If we do not accomplish this work we will receive one hundred different troubles. If we accomplish what he said sincerely then we will be able to hope to reach him, and if we are sinful and stubborn, danger will certainly come upon us. No tribe has a shah like this. To live without him is equal to a thousand sufferings.'

VII

After Hoopoe Told the Legend about Semurgh, the Birds Desire was on Fire

These words inspired the birds and each of them got excited about the possibilities. They said to Hoopoe,

'O leader! It is impossible to live without such a shah. He is aware of all of our situations. We should not be overcome by ignorance when we have such a shah living. We have been separated from him and so we are desperate to reach him. Every wise and aware person sees this clearly in front of them. It is much better to die than to live in ignorance.

'By your words you have showed us the way. Now we have a favor to ask of you. Be our leader and guide us in this journey. For the shah, our spirits we should submit, even by the handful, along with our tears and youth. Let us try to meet him and not give up our dream for one moment. Let us fly over any deserts and seas. Either let us meet him or let us relinquish our spirits on the way.'

VIII

Hoopoe Alights and Fosters the Journey

Being joyful of the birds' words Hoopoe replied:

'O my depressed flock! If heaven helps us to reach happiness, and if you really want to embark on this trip, this trip will also have my whole heart. Perhaps my physical strength will remain until I have finished helping you. Let me sympathize with whatever sorrow you have on the way. If there are hidden anxieties let me be the confidant. If you come across any problems let me solve them with my heart. If you encounter all kinds of good and evil let me always be ready to drive it away. Let me be the companion when you fly and the guard when you land.'

When he saw that they understood all that he said he praised and blessed them. Although fatigued he began speaking of different secrets one by one.

'All of you want to know these secrets. Even your descendents have admired this hidden treasure. From the beginning of your creation you had pleasant poems and tunes in the branches of the garden of paradise, and all of you wanted to be a confidant of the shah's secrets. Your pleasant singing is from his rosary and your songs and poems commemorate him.

'His remembrance of you is always joyful and likewise you pass the time by remembering and thinking of him. However, when a low character abruptly startled your flock the bright candle became hidden from your eyes. Rebellion reached the flock because of this. Every one of you became troubled and destitute. You could not find the direction of the flower garden. Perhaps your greed was too much. It was evident that you were inclined to the godless garden.

'You had been stable in this impoverished land, but the lowly one had a merry time of taking the pride and good fruit of your heart. With truth's help I will quickly try to undo it. You have been his like-minded friend too long. In this trek you will have to patiently endure difficulty and suffering. If your heart withstands him you will cross over to the final goal. If you are victorious your body's spirit will be pure. Your state will once again reach its first radiance. You will know and partake of the shahdom, and your soul will live eternally. You will know suffering and with the shah be aware of the folly of your lusts.'

IX

Hoopoe Appeals to the Parrot and Exhorts Him to Fulfill his Purpose

'O one who is famous for his language, offer a song. Sing sweet-tongued Parrot! Seek the king with your green coat and show the way for the lost ones as Hizr![11]

'First of all remember the ultimate place where you are to go and make your heart hopeful with the thought of the shah. Your dear motherland was India. You lived in a special garden of the king. There you ate sweets and your words were nectarous. Your singing was the luscious meeting place of lovers. The king's hand provided your dwelling and final resting place. He served as the object of your speech. Now leave from that alien land and fly towards the blooming flowers!'

X

Hoopoe Gives a Beautiful Address to the Peacock

'O Peacock, who for eons has made people inebriated, show us your elegance! You have the crown of leadership on your head. Your body is majestic and a field of loveliness. Your body and face are so beautiful that the tongue has no words to describe it. You have been created for goodness. Your kind was born to be someone's sweetheart. However, you seem to have forgotten your own place and the brilliant garden near the shah. Never forget that paradise. Abandon this field of ruins and prison. Fly towards the shah's beautiful garden so that you can take part in his gathering!'

XI

Hoopoe Sings using the Nightingale's Melody

'O Nightingale, that is the pleasure of the flower garden. Sing loudly so that the tunes of your song will let out pleasure's wonderful secrets!

---

[11] One who found 'the water of life' and obtained its power. In literature Hizr is described as a guide who suddenly appears to help those who have lost their way. Hizr is a symbol of good deeds and wisdom.

Compose a thousand varieties of love tunes and start a song of solemnity! Being intoxicated from the flower's beauty in the shah's garden, raise a toast that will make you drunk of this flower's love. During the merry spring while the flaming flowers are radiant, let its every petal be reflected in your feather.

'However, you are now far from the fresh flower garden. The experience of separation has turned your body to ash. Fly towards the deep blue sky. Towards that very red flower you want to see. Hundreds of flowers shimmer in the shah's garden, but here you still are burning beside the light of separation!'

XII

Hoopoe Sings using the Turtledove's Mode

'O Turtledove of the garden, sing a song about your life. With your marvelous tunes make the flock of birds speechless and powerless. You have accepted a rosary of reeds that cannot be properly described. For amongst every garden you wander harassed. Sometimes you are smeared with blood and sometimes you are muddied. Sometimes you seem mad with love's woe and you groan sorrowfully. As you recall the garden of lovers you become baffled. The good news for you is this; drop your troubles and rise swiftly towards that flower garden.'

XIII

Hoopoe Sings in the Way of the Partridge

'O Partridge from the mountain of sorrow! Let your eyes burn in sorrow like the ruby and let it charm others with your beauty. Start taking big strides like Farhad[12] who does not stay in one place. Your beak is red like tulips. This is a clear proof of your great suffering. Qof is on your mind and yet you stay far from it. You are wailing from a distance. This loud singing is not joyful laughter, but perhaps the bitter laughter of your

---

[12] Farhad represents a senseless lover in Central Asian literature. Nava'i wrote his own epic poem ('Farhad and Shirin') on the famous romantic.

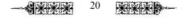

mourning. You have now dared to move towards Qof mountain. Therefore, be hopeful to attain its joy. The hope of meeting is imminent. Cheer up and cast aside the stone that is "separation mountain"!'

XIV

When the Pheasant Swayed Beautifully Hoopoe Began Singing about the Journey

'O beautiful Pheasant who proudly coquettes! Your laughter belongs in the well-tended main garden. Your beauty bestows charm to the garden and even the flowers feel embarrassed before the blush of your face. You shimmer whether in the garden or the grassland. They take pride in your beauty. You are the favorite of those who belong to the flowers and the pleasure of wild animals. However, do not be proud of your beauty even though it is indescribable. Remember Semurgh and move like ravenous fire towards the flower garden!'

XV

Hoopoe Struts in the Way of the Pheasant

'Come, come, O Pheasant! You are extremely beautiful. You are pleasing to everyone like a beloved bird. You are the highlight of the woods. With your every step green grass grows more. Your soothing songs tug the heart; its listeners are ready to forget everything. You are beautiful and your figure is attractive and desirable. The form of your shape and speech is incomparable. You are pleasing to see and charming. With your beautiful and fluid singing you should first of all free yourself of this chain. You are worth being hunted by that shah. When he traps you, give yourself to him and you will enjoy eternal life.'

XVI

Hoopoe Flies Like a Pigeon

'O pigeon! Fly into the sky. Strike the high heaven there and show us all kinds of motions. Do not keep sitting in the dark room of your own house!

You became blind by continually sitting in your nest, didn't you? Dream now of reaching the shah's castle. Flap your wings harder to fulfill this hope. You seem to have given up thinking of flying high and alighting on the roof of the shah's castle. You have completely forgotten about the height of your position and the expediency of alighting on the roof of his castle. In the presence of the castle's sultan remember the royal music, as you are completely exalted. Start in that direction now! Land on that roof and be happy on top of the world. Perhaps he will accept you into his presence. You should be able to find the way to the sweet khan of pigeons!'

XVII

The Falcon's Beauty and Hoopoe's Guidance

'How beautiful you are, O king-like falcon! Both your appearance and face are very beautiful. Among the true birds you are truly proud. You taught all remaining birds how to be beautiful. The shah's hand has always served as your nest. He has always found food to feed you. With his hand he has caressed your wings and held onto your beak and claws. Meanwhile something has brought in discord and you are separated from the shah. Once the snare of division afflicted you, your disposition quickly became accustomed to lonely days. Now think of the shah again and reach a high rank by kissing his hand!'

XVIII

Hoopoe Sings a Song of Praise Describing the Falcon as a Shah

'O Falcon who made the high sky and the shah's hand your place, welcome! Among the birds you are one who seems to have a crown just like the shahs. The shah considered it suitable to have a golden crown placed on your head. You are leader of the crowned birds. For this reason the shah is willing to talk with you. At his feast you will have the highest seat and be shown much respect and attention. On the basis of your courage, in the midst of strangers, the shah has allowed your destiny to be ten times better than others. With his hand he favorably strokes your neck and decorates it with pearls and diamonds. You, however, are quite far from your dear

shah. Put this separation aside now and alight on his hand to make that place your homeland!'

XIX

The Birds Start Out and Some Encounter Difficulties

Hoopoe openly told the birds about love's secrets. He sang the language of the birds and set in motion thoughts of union and separation. The birds felt awkward about their state of separation and had a hundred sweet dreams of union. Each of them thought of their lowly state of their separation. Their lengthy amnesia of union and their torment of separation propelled them. They realized how far they were from happiness and where they had gone astray. What Hoopoe said made them aware that they were ignorant and had lost their way. They felt deeply that they were far away from love and in the vortex of separation. Realizing this they suffered so much that everybody could notice it. Each one was so ashamed that they were ready to leave their lives. They were ashamed of their deeds and were depressed about their group's behavior.

Although they suffered much they tried to forget about what had been done and decided to fly towards the shah day and night while they were still alive. They decided not to give up the idea of flying towards the shah no matter how many various difficulties they would meet in the valley of demand or how much they would suffer on the road.

All the birds were united and met to harmonize over the speech and their long separation. They wholeheartedly agreed with Hoopoe and he became the guide of the flock that was ready to start. They started off happy and flew off into the sky in the hope of sweet union.

Everyday on the way they flew over wasteland. As the journey continued they faced a lot of difficulties, setbacks, trials, grief, and torture. The weak suffered various misfortunes.

Formerly they had spent their days proudly in the gardens, enjoying the cool shade of the trees during the hot summers. They missed their old peaceful life, and they yearned for their tranquil orchards and gardens. They recalled the happy times, the relaxing nooks, and the revelry of the gardens.

('Farhad and Shirin') on the famous romantic.

On the way some of the birds became wounded and began to despise the journey. In feebleness they asked leave from Hoopoe. One by one they expressed their excuses. These excuses seemed reasonable to them and so they left the journey in a hundred different directions. All of them made this request to Hoopoe:

'O our leader, stop for a moment! Some of us are so desolate. Some of our souls have become sick from wandering on this journey. Some have various problems; therefore, they want you to help them. They have something they want to tell you. Their speech is full of the melody of suffering. It is necessary for them to inform you otherwise they will be unable to continue.'

Having seen their frailty Hoopoe gathered all of them in one place. He alighted in a valley to listen to their malady and said:

'Well now, whoever has something to say - say it.'

XX

The Parrot's Excuse

First of all the parrot began to say his excuse. He spoke the following of his weakness:

'I am the bird who meanders in warm countries like India. For my eloquent speech, my fame has spread all over the world. I comfort sad people with my words. The cage of happy, rich people has been my abode. They keep me from all kinds of hardships. From the hands of gorgeous girls I take food. They nurture me with sugar and sweets. Occasionally I am face to face with a girl who resembles the moon. In my life I have seen nothing but gladness. My speech bestows one hundred kinds of happiness to people. Ever since I was conscious of myself, I have never met hardship nor known what sorrow means. The place you have talked about is the place where the eagle is equal to the fly. How can we who are weaker than a fly get there? I will never know how to fly in that direction! I cannot think of how I can go the distance like the other birds! In such a situation do you think it is possible for me to accompany you! For one moment look at me!'

XXI

Hoopoe's Answer to the Parrot

Hoopoe gave him this answer:

'All your words are lies, and consist of mistakes and contradictions. You think that your foolish talking is eloquence. You calculate your lowly speech as maturity. You praised yourself and what you said contradicts it in every way. All that you have said is fabricated. They are nothing but lies and exaggeration. You are egotistical in your thinking; therefore you are given over to wickedness. You were proud of your eloquence and the image in the mirror in front of you. Yet, in reality your words deserve mockery and laughter. A real mirror can endure a hundred difficulties and bring sheen to the surface of the land.

'You said that every Hindu seems to be a shah. This is also false. In reality your shah is the very one from whom you are turning away. You have strayed from the way. The words you are saying are senseless in every way. In the apology you gave, your arguments are irrational. Ignorance and deception impede your heart's awareness. If you awaken from you state and open your eyes you will understand how bad your state is. However, late regrets will not do you any good. You will be very sorry for what you have done and ashamed of what you have said. What you believe is not real. On account of your lusts Satan has ridiculed your species.'

XXII

An Exemplary Story

An ignorant man whose existence was dependent on improper desires walked into the market. He had a green coat on like the one Hizr used to wear and his lust was satisfied by that green color.

In the shops he saw many goods and could not refrain from the temptation of tasting them. In his gluttony his temptations edged him on. He skillfully portrayed himself as a beggar and in the crowds he began saying various things about himself. Sometimes he spoke of the perfection he had reached, and sometimes he spoke about his legendary foretelling. Sometimes he boasted about how wisely he obeyed the rules of Shari'at.

Thus, using hundreds of tricks and deceits he obtained food and money from people. By following his wicked temptations, he cheated himself and others. Every time, after taking drugs, he was taken to one hundred bad dreams and idiotic thoughts were placed in his mind.

Suddenly at such a time a mature person who was experienced and had traveled the world came to him. Seeing the sly man he immediately altered his own bad state.

The person said, 'In front of the religious leader show the things you have obtained. What do you have to show for yourself? What have you accomplished?'

He opened and showed his sack to this greedy and astute person. It was full of toxic things. After the inquisitor saw all the dirty things he had collected, he became very angry and his heart was tormented. This leader took a handful of mud and stones and gave them to him. 'Look at them!' he said. When he looked at his hand he suddenly saw that the mud had turned into gold, and the stones into diamonds and precious pearls. As soon as the deceitful man saw it the mature leader who was standing before him disappeared. He was so disgraced among the people that he felt very ashamed. However, what is the use of passing on such bewilderment and cries to the sky?

'O Parrot, the words that you said are like that. Your words remind us precisely of that green coat person's situation.'

XXIII

The Peacock's Excuse

Then the Peacock began his plea and said:

'O leader of all of us! I am the bird who beautifies palaces and gardens. The people of the world are dumbfounded by my designs and colors. If my beauty decorates the garden then one who sees my moving will be given to peace. Because of me gardens flourish during the times of falling leaves. The forests become flower gardens in the winter. If I make graceful movements and shake out my wings, from head to foot it will be like a mirror that reveals all that is happening in the world.[13]

---

[13] 'Iskandar's mirror' – Alexander the Great made a mirror by polishing iron, from which everything happening in the world could be seen.

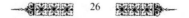

'God conferred to me limitless beauty and more than enough elegant jewelry so that people could gaze at my beauty and praise his power. For God has created each person for something: one is created to taste honey and another is created to be stung. Therefore, people try to work wisely and everyone tries to see what their destiny has prepared for them. If the fairy is pleasant by God's order then Satan is sentenced to unhappiness. No person can go outside of God's order for them, and one cannot resist any other suggestion.'

XXIV

Hoopoe's Answer to the Peacock

In answer Hoopoe caught his breath and then said:

'O one who belongs to ignorant people and envies everything! You have described situations that may come only to demented people and young children. One should not speak about external beauty. Whoever is proud of himself does not belong to people. Pride and beauty is only for beloved girls. A man is good when he has pain and hardships. For all created beings the most glorious work is this: to move from form to meaning. You cherish your form and that is why you are worth being laughed at in the midst of people. For people should not be proud of their external beauty. If they are proud of it then they deserve to be mocked!'

XXV

A Story

A Hindu tried various means to reveal interesting spectacles. Finally, the clown put a notched crown on top of his head. His crown and clothes looked like gold because they were comprised of a shiny yellow substance and bronze. He had a throng of Hindu kettledrum players and singers around him. They danced shaking their arms and heads in an Indian style. They looked very beautiful as if they were the ornament of the garden and they glimmered just like an Indian peacock.

In this way the clown display bedazzled the square. An unruly crowd surrounded him. His group was filled with turmoil. At that moment security

informants arrived and the circle of people fled in all directions. Having been a swindler and boaster the Indian was apprehended. His kettledrum and crown were broken and his bare body was beaten with a thick whip. In this way his 'art' served as an example for people. Also, this fate became the 'decoration' for his crown.

XXVI

The Nightingale's Excuse

The nightingale said:

'O one who orders this meeting! I have traveled far from the flower of my universe. Having been parted with my lover and mystic I have lost my place. Intelligence, awareness and patience have become foreign to me. Without her I have neither patience nor endurance! I am in such a predicament, O comrade, how I can endure separation from her! Why is it that when the flower in the garden shines I am merry and give commentary on my own secrets to it with one thousand different songs? With her love my impulsiveness increases with each moment and her beauty continually surprises me. After she leaves the garden I suddenly become deaf and dumb and even too weak to start singing a song. I am sedate with the memory of her in the garden. When I am separated from her I suffer one hundred problems. She is the only one in my heart, in my soul, and in my consciousness. She is under my watch and guard.

'One should look at the shah with a perfect face. As the lover of a flower, there is no way for me to do this!'

XXVII

Hoopoe's Answer to the Nightingale

After hearing the tale Hoopoe said the following:

'Do not keep making so much clatter about your love! What you have said is not love, but from top to bottom it is fantasy. Enough already! Listen, after this dream there is no news. Stop speaking about it! In the world nobody is ignorant like you who bows down to evil desires.

'You have forced yourself to be seen as a lover and raised all kinds of racket about love. In a year a flower only blossoms about five days and in

ten days falls to the ground. Is this great fuss for one who does not last long in the garden? Only to be strewn and not devoted to? It is good to not be in love with this kind of beauty. It is not worth loving. You should consider love to be that which will live long and not wither no matter how weak it is. Although this love of yours may seem to be true love to you, it will end horribly.'

XXVIII

A Story

Once a king was traveling by horseback and a boastful beggar saw him and fell in love with him. He began crying and disturbing the people around him. Just like you, he had to do a thousand different laments. Like a lunatic he could not remain stationary but would dirty himself with ash.

When the king found out about this love and insanity he wanted to test it. One day he was riding his adorned horse and directed it to the bonfire where the beggar was lying. The king ordered his men: 'Drag that erroneous man to me and behead him in my presence!' When the beggar was dragged along the ground to the king, his dream was fulfilled. He had reached his love's aim. Then the cheery king pronounced his death sentence. The beggar panicked. Adverse he glanced back and began running away. Since he was terrified he did not know where to run. People chased after him to catch him. Gasping he ran towards the bonfire. Not knowing what to do he threw himself into the fire and burned.

This is the purpose of the shah's test: if the beggar were a true lover he would have remained loyal to his judgment and accepted the death sentence. In that case the shah would have descended his horse asked for his forgiveness and found out about his condition. In return for his loyalty the shah would have made him his companion and part of his family. Regardless, the beggar's love was false and that is why his dishonorable state became notorious.

'If a thorn from that beloved flower harms you too, your home will not be a garden but a bonfire.'

XXIX

The Turtledove's Excuse

The Turtledove said:

'O wise one, the guide of the lost and ignorant ones! I'm such a bird that in my life I have always had flowers around me and have never tired myself out by traveling whole steppes and valleys. I am known for my weakness. I build my nest among the branches and leaves of trees. In the world I have neither seen cold nor heat. Neither has my head faced suffering nor hardships. From this garden to that garden and from this branch to that branch I always move and have merry times. In such a case, how can I keep caring for such a difficult journey and be fit to ascend its tribulations? If my spirit leaves for these troubles, will I not be forced to spill my own blood?'

XXX

Hoopoe's Answer to the Turtledove

The Hoopoe said to him:

'O Turtledove who has fallen face down with weakness! Sorrow and pleasure are considered proper for your heart. Even if you stay in the gardens thousands of years and fly amongst the branches and leaves, what will your travels yield? Inevitably, a cat lies in wait on your way and will snag you, rip open your abdomen and drink your blood. Or some weapon's shot could kill you or a stray stone take your soul. Besides, the taste of the revelry that you have mentioned back there is nothing. If this is the respect that the garden shows you, then I think it would be better to die fighting as a real hero than to be ignorant. Search for your intimate lover. If you sacrifice your soul along the way, and die with troubles and hardship, there will be nothing to mourn. Until now your situation has deserved shame, and death is a hundred times better than that.'

XXXI

A Story

There was a pupil who was a gardener. However, he did not know anything about the art of gardening. He did not know how to graft trees or how to make use of the fruits. He did not know how to tend the trees, or when the flowers and grains were to be planted. He was simply happy with making and picking hay in the garden. Actually he should be labeled a haymaker and not a gardener. In this way he suffered and his life was wasted. His friends advised him to forsake such barren work and console himself with useful work. However, he did not listen to them at all. The foolish gardener did not relinquish the difficult work with which he was busy. One day as he was trimming the vines a snake bit him. He died.

XXXII

The Pigeon's Excuse

Then the Pigeon explained the circumstances of his excuse:
'O master of perfection in showing the route of the way! Of all the birds God honored me by allowing me to eat food from the hands of people. They build dwellings and palaces for me and place water and grain in front of me. In the world I am the prisoner of their traps, and so I have quickly learned to be accustomed to them. This destiny is given to me from God's rich tablecloth. It seems that truth has allowed this. How can I refuse it since it corresponds with his wise law? Shouldn't I thank God that I do not give up on this difficult life?'

XXXIII

Hoopoe's Answer to the Pigeon

Hoopoe said to him.
'O one who is a professional finder of various excuses! The nest of deceit and slyness seems to be your place. The birds were surprised by this state of yours. It is impossible to find a passive one like you. God destined you to fly all over the world and have powerful wings. And there

you are, sitting in front of the people needy and fidgety. You are captive to the water and grain given by the people. People would tie a rag onto the end of a stick and chase after your flock! They keep you from their roofs and drive away your useless flock. Despite the great harm they show you, with avariciousness you show your face near them. You cannot go anywhere but from one piece of their roof to another.'

XXXIV

A Story

There was a loafer who lived among the people. People were surprised by his apathy. People beat, slapped, and kicked him. In exchange for this he received a chunk of bread or food. This was his way of living. Although people drove him away he would not go anywhere else and would not abandon his bad habits. Every torture that he endured had a certain price. From whoever kicked or punched him he would require something to eat that would be suitable to the torture given.

One day someone gave him a piece of bread and beat him so hard that he fell down and remained still on the ground. Although he used to stuff himself with slaps in the face, with one blow he bit the ground.

XXXV

The Mountain Partridge's Excuse

Once again, the mountain partridge displayed weakness and said:

'O leader of all birds! I'm the bird who makes his home in the mountains. Out there my tongue is busy praising God. In this manner I shook off the people and found peace and pleasure at the foot of the mountain. As I already had a high desire to be a hermit I became happy and the treasure of the mountain became my sanctuary. This is how it is. Is it right to leave my place for such a journey? After always having been around the mines what I now desire are diamonds. It is still difficult to obtain spiritual diamonds. This route is meaningless to me; it is nothing but a trip!'

XXXVI

Hoopoe's Answer to the Mountain Partridge

Hoopoe replied:

'O one who is given to empty dreams! Your pride is nothing but empty dreams. You said that on the mountain you are a hermit and far from people. Actually it is not a remote place; you are just given to lust and the sky. Over the mountains and peaks you fly to and fro without stopping. It is useless to laugh all the time like a crazy person. Also, you spoke inappropriately about spiritual diamonds. You have become drunk with anger and only think about yourself. Where are you and where is your spirituality! Do not knave with various lies and do not open your mouth about your meaningful diamond! By your words you have proved to be of low breeding, foolish and pitiful. You have been afflicted with such lies that a hundred disasters are sure to come upon your head.'

XXXVII

A Story

There was a man who was a lowly swindler. He went to the city and called himself an expert appraiser of precious stones. Yet, he could not distinguish donkey beads from sapphires. Greedily he produced false diamonds as best as he could and left his begging. He smeared different colors with pieces of glass and slyly called them sapphire and ruby. People thought his fraudulent work to be real. One day that fraud showed his craft to a rich man and exorbitantly sold an ordinary piece of stone that he had painted a good color. Before long he spent all the money.

The man who bought the stone found out that it was a fake. The swindler had sold him a ruby glass for one hundred thousand pieces. The owner of the stone went back and proceeded to buy another one but stopped halfway, caught the fraud, and demanded his money back. However, the impostor had no money to give him. Therefore, they tortured and killed the swindler.

XXXVIII

The Pheasant's Excuse

The beautiful Pheasant gave the following complaint:
'O one who is famous for showing the right way! I am a bird that possesses beauty. I look incredibly beautiful in the garden. God granted me incomparable beauty from the beginning. God designed my enduring and incomparable beauty. With my endless beauty I am dearly loved among the people. Don't you think that one who is dear among the people should coquette since people do not want beauties to be sorrowful?'

XXXIX

Hoopoe's Answer to the Pheasant

Hoopoe said:
'O bird with good thoughts, dispositions, words and discipline! Nobody is so proud of his beauty and exaggerates as you do. Even lunatics, simple people, and babies do not say these words. Even whores who dress with various colors are ashamed of your words. No one has ever made such vain claims. Men and even hermaphrodites will not make these kinds of assertions! It is better for one not to do this journey if he expresses his perfection even though he is weak. You look like the women who prize themselves. In this case people are ashamed of your name. Humanity is respected for its kindness. The person who is proud of his adornments is not a person. A person's real beauty is in their good behavior. Such a person will not care if something is a golden robe or an old rug.'

XL

A Story

Two friends were going along the road. One of them had a thorough knowledge of Sufism and the second one did not know his way. One of them possessed a quality of perfection and the second one had a lot of shortcomings. The first one's father's name was 'Fortunate' and

the other one's was 'Unfortunate'. Their names suited their quality and the quality was apt for their name. If the fortunate father spoke rightly about Allah's household, saints, and knowledgeable people, the unfortunate father went on only about unbelievers and sin's household. If this man spoke about those in suffering the second one babbled about appearance. They continued on their way without enjoying each other. When a beautiful city appeared before them, the companions seized the opportunity and quickly separated. The fortunate man went to the street where Sufis stayed and the unfortunate man went to the whorehouse.

The king of the country came to see the fortunate man paying one hundred respects. While the king was talking with him a group of people dragged the unfortunate man before him and complained about his bad behavior. They said that a band of hooligans had become drunk and had gone carousing. One of them said to the unfortunate man 'You're ugly' and so the bastard stabbed and killed him. After listening to this, the king gave justice and brought retribution upon the man.

In conclusion, the humble man received an opportunity to speak with the king and obtained high status. The selfish man, however, found punishment. Truly the spark will rise towards the high sky, while a gleaming fly will remain atop rubbish.

XLI

The Hawk's Excuse

Showing his claws and beak the Hawk spoke:
'I do not look like other birds, but I am considered to be the master of perhaps all birds. So far all the birds that have spoken and asked for leave are my food. I rest in the shah's' hand and everyday he provides for me. If I spread my wings to attack any bird they become my prey. Even if it is a flying eagle it is unlikely that it will escape me. Such is the respect that I have among the shahs. The validity of my glory is doubtless and is not less than Semurgh's. After having the shah's hand as my throne and a crown on my head, I do not need to fly towards Semurgh!'

XLII

Hoopoe's Answer to the Hawk

Hoopoe replied:

'O bird that has become corrupt under the influence of pride and has become low with anger and ignorance! You should know this: it is easy for the shah to keep you under his control let alone for a simple hunter to do so. You are caught in his presence. On the account of hunger and insomnia your flesh sticks to your bones. You are so impatient and cry out until someone puts a piece of meat in front of you. You need people of low breed and to spend your days in misery and need. What God has given is what you have to eat. Whenever you are able to catch something to eat the hunter will immediately play the kettledrum and chase you. You always attack ones weaker than you. In hunger you hunt them. You submit to your master and deliver your prey to him. You spend your days giving food to the bird-keeper. Aren't you ashamed of lying, exaggerations, and your pitiful state? If you had the least bit of conscience or shame, you would think it better to die than have this disgraceful life. However, ignorance remains in you. Obviously, your lusts have made you inclined to talk foolishly.'

XLIII

A Story

Once a mountaineer caught a mountain bear and suffered long to tame him. The former roaming bear had been beaten with sticks twice a day. Hunger and limitless blows had made his life awful. That's why when his master showed a stick the bear meekly obeyed him. The bear danced in the streets and brought firewood to his master's house. His lord loaded excessive cargo on him and from the continuous burdens the bears' shoulders had no fur left. He endured every possible suffering and misfortune that existed in the world. However, since the bear was ignorant he became haughty in his thoughts. Sometimes he thought he would crush the leopard's head by his cunningness and spite. Sometimes he would think that he would boldly tear off the terrible lion's stomach if he met him. His various raw thoughts took on these characteristics. In the end, he became fodder for the dogs.

'You are exactly in that useless bear's circumstances since you speak foolishly among the people.'

XLIV

The Falcon's Excuse

The Falcon spoke:

'O leader of the flock that has submitted to his order! God has honored me and created me stronger than all other birds. All shahs are proud of me. They call me the king of birds because I was bestowed a golden helmet.[14] My golden crown is on my head. You know very well about my conditions and my breed and name among the birds. Is it good to search for a king if one has a crown on his head? Why should I submit to a shah when I am a shah myself?'

XLV

Hoopoe's Answer to the Falcon

Hoopoe replied:

'O poor slow-witted one! Your thoughts will increase dread in your group. You are concerned about saying that you are a shah - it is nothing but vain thoughts. Many black people are really black and yet they are called 'white' among people. The notions of 'sultan' and 'shah' are widespread among people, and even people of lower class use these titles for themselves. Not every person becomes a man when he says he is a man, right? Can one say he will accomplish the work when he is unable? Only ignorant people call you shah. It is like naming an idol or fire 'God'. You are comparable to a chess king. Who is such a shah that every mean and petty man who wants can raise him to the sky in a flash and then strike him to the ground.

'The difference between your shah likeness and the shah is the difference between ground and sky. It is a thousand times better to be a beggar than to claim to have shahdom.'

---

[14] The metal cap that is used for trained hunting falcons in Central Asia.

XLVI

A Story

A king gave a big party for the whole country and wanted to have a good spread. The splendor of it greatly exceeded their expectations. Everyone in the country and cities adorned themselves from head to foot and began to amble around. At this party the artists displayed their mastery. They erected one hundred shining four cornered domed tents that resembled the sun. The craftsmen decorated all the tents so well that they became the beauty of the whole country. Many marvels were discovered so that life itself was adorned in magic. Everyone tried to become merry and play tricks. In order to forget their grief they had great partying.

A detestable person proclaimed himself to be the king of straw. On top of his clothes from head to foot there was straw. He had fashioned his bag, shield, and banner also from straw. Some of his unscrupulous joker friends dress up the same way. Dressed like this he came upon the square where the feast was held. On their way they introduced all kinds of bad and blasphemous games. Their leader considered himself the country's king and whatever jests they made he took seriously.

At last the joyful holiday came to an end and the scoundrel consoled himself. He was caught. They struck down his fan and the crown from his head and his grass robe was destroyed and burnt. He realized then that his shahdom was nothing but a farce.

XLVII

The Eagle's Excuse

The Eagle, the Eagle himself, came to the middle and said:

'O master of the birds! My situation is not like other birds. People don't laud me or describe me like the Turtledove or the Nightingale. My magnificence is huge and my fury is terrifying. I am the hero of the mountain country. Every day several quails are my food. If I don't have them my eyes won't sleep at night. If I rise to the sky and search for food, there is no way wild donkeys[15] or deer can elude me. How can a bird with

---

[15] 'Kulon' – An Asian wild donkey.

such a big throat continue on its way without food? Imagine me flapping my wings for a long time on this road, after my stomach is empty they will count me as having fallen.'

XLVIII

Hoopoe's Answer to the Eagle

Hoopoe replied:

'O powerful ruler! The people of the world, even until now, have not seen a bird like you! Your breed is worthy of humanity's praise and your horse is worthy of being powerful. Now then, isn't it a shame for you to have these claws and beak with glorious wings! O glutton and scoundrel! Follow your original purpose! Don't show such weakness before the journey. You stay not taking to the road and draw your wings to the side. Is this not a shame for your claws, beak and wings? You described yourself by them, didn't you? You yourself described your greatness and glory, didn't you? Be certain of this, the one who let's his dear life go will be seen as truly powerful and heroic.'

XLIX

A Story

Once there was a brave man who was unique in ineptness. He used to stuff himself mid-morning and in the evening make himself eat that much food again. In the course of these two events he would take in that much food again. He was so strong that he could even hurt low standing elephants. Suddenly, because of a crisis, destruction appeared in the country.

Therefore, the local people abandoned their places and were compelled to flee in many directions. Being unaware of the difficulties of the road the brave man accompanied them. The road was long and for the gluttonous people there were no well-to-do places to satisfy their cravings.

In just the first day with not having eaten anything the brave man entered a state of mourning. The second day his body's strength did not hold up. The third day that poor man was forced to yield his life in the wasteland.

After another two or three days of having dragged themselves through

hardship young children and even two hunch-backed elders reached the final place. They came to the well-to-do place and achieved their purposes. As for the brave one, he could not endure the suffering, and death destroyed him on the way.

L

The Owl's Excuse

The Owl made the following appeal about his state:

'I am a weak, poor bird and the road is too dangerous. I have spent my life in a ruined place that was ready to fall down on my head. Sadness and sorrow have afflicted my whole life; like people with abiding sorrow I experience soft lamenting. Hoping to obtain the treasure under the ruins I wail a lot and even lose consciousness. I have suffered so much that it is no wonder that one day in my destiny there will be gold. I am neurotic in hope of the treasure. Day and night I have made the ruins my place to dwell. Don't try to persuade me to go this long way! Where am I? Where is Semurgh and Qof Mountain?'

LI

Hoopoe's Answer to the Owl

Hoopoe answered:

'O bird that consists of only wrongdoings and tricks! With your deeds you are attempting assassination on your soul. It is impossible to fulfill what is in your heart. Only empty dreams have been formed. It is not possible to have them accepted.

'O frail collector of problems, suppose that in your case you found a treasure. Even then numerous misfortunes would pour down upon your head and you would receive all new sorrows. You will die in the vortex of this evil, with its assaults and disasters, and the treasure will pass on to your enemy.'

LII

A Story

There was a demented man in a country. His dwelling, day and night, was a ruin. Every day he dug around it. During his life he hoped to find some treasure. All of a sudden after suffering from much hardship he got lucky and found treasure. While he was digging in the hole he saw a door. Once he entered inside he saw a huge palace. Here there were forty crocks that equaled Faridun's[16] treasure, no, perhaps it was equal with Qorun's.[17] Seeing the vast riches the man fainted. Meanwhile a scoundrel came in. He saw the unconscious lunatic lying in front of the treasure and without any hesitation he stabbed him and spilled his blood.

His life's aim was to acquire a treasure, however, for all of his wealth he became separated from his life.

LIII

The Phoenix's Excuse

The honorable Phoenix began his apology this way:

'O leader of all roaming birds! I'm so happy in the world, since I can bestow people glorious thrones with my shadow. If God granted my kind such glory, that even my shadow makes the pauper rise to a shah, what need is there for me to wish to be yet another shah? Why should I set my sights on making myself have difficulties? Would it not be better for me to give shelter to the shahs with my wings and fly in the sky?'

---

[16] Faridun or Afridun – a king who belonged to the Peshdodi dynasty of ancient Iran. When Faridun joined the rebellion of Kova-Kovain, he killed Zahhok who was a very cruel and bloodthirsty king. Faridun was famous for his honorable behavior, justice and having a large treasury.

[17] Qorun belonged to an old Jewish clan and is legendary for owning an unbelievable amount of treasure, but he was very greedy. Qorun's name symbolizes richness and greediness in Persian literature.

LIV

Hoopoe's Answer to the Phoenix

Hoopoe replied:

'These words of yours are nothing but a myth. What you have said only neurotic people are able to say. According to what you have said, it is as if you are of a high breed and very glorious, as if you raise people to shahdom with your shadow! Are you that far-gone? If you look through the history of shahs, you will notice nothing like this has ever happened. Is there anyone who has been conferred a shah by your shadow? This erroneous myth has made you happy and you have believed such corrupt values.

'For example, in the event that what you asserted was true and that quality was upon you, what good is it if the person who passed under your shadow became a shah by God's power? Regardless, like a dog you have bones, that is, bones that have been gnawed and dried out in the desert, and you live on them, don't you?

'O you have been held captive to a broken dream. If you understand this, then in your case it can serve as a good example.'

LV

A Story

There are many that are busy with trade by the seashore. At the seaboard many tradesmen striving to get rich meet each other. They give the petty divers five or ten dirham hoping to get a big profit. Those divers have suffered a hundred sorrows in their soul seeking for pearls in the depths of the sea. Whether they find one thousand pearls or ones that are remarkable enough to decorate king's crowns, regardless, they give the diver standard pay and count the pearls as their property. In this way the tradesmen obtain real pearls and the divers continue to be the owners of nothing but small change.

'The diver receives his payment and gets a little, however, you poor creature won't get anything. Like a dog you keep being satisfied with a bone. If you are wise, then don't speak vain words; for all of your words contradict truth.'

LVI

The Duck's Excuse

The Duck began his words like this:

'O happy one! My life is alive with water. If I get separated from it, just like a fish far from water I will be immersed in grief. My breed has peace of mind in water. That's why it is customary for me to wash myself clean. Through water I have gained purity. Therefore, it has become appropriate to characterize me as an owner of beauty. If I am not in pure water for just a second I will be distraught due to separation. In the waves of the water I have laid my prayer mat and in that mirror reflects my purpose. My original aim is to be on the water. That's enough! To want to fly somewhere else is, for me, a mistake.'

LVII

Hoopoe's Answer to the Duck

Hoopoe replied:

'All of what you have said is full of mistakes. The water has quite washed off your intelligence. You said you have laid a prayer mat on the water. Perhaps you were unaware of the Owl's lot? Do not exaggerate saying that in the water you are always pure. Also, in the water do not consider yourself free from sin. If you are really pure then why do you keep diving into the water day and night? Whoever for their lust splashes about in depravity should dive deep into the water to be free of them. What kind of circumstance is this: you dive into the water day and night and have not become pure? If you are a real man go dive in the sea of nothingness that is in front of you and mingle with your beloved!'

LVIII

A Story

There was a tradesman by the Indian Ocean who was skillful in business dealings. He felt that he was so well established in business that he did not think of sinking in the water at all. He would not stay more than ten

days in a country. As soon as he finished his business he would take to the water. He thought that the sea was free of any danger and for years he traveled like this. Despite passing around Mecca many times in the water, even after having been near, he returned not fulfilling his duty. People would tell him that he should do the Hajj and fulfill his duty. However, his greed for money did not let the tradesman go further.

One day a storm rose up on the sea. The boat he had boarded leapt to the sky and then fell low several times. As the tradesman had sank into his business so the boat sank into the sea. The thought of swimming in the sea did not allow him to go on the Hajj. As a result, he became food for a big fish.

LIX

The Rooster's Pardon

The Rooster explained his plight this way:

'O chairman of the birds and owner of a crown! God has provided both of us with a crown, but each one of us has been designated different tasks. You were given guidance and the right to be the birds' chairman and religious leader. He gave me a captivating tune to continually call people to prayer in the early morning and in the evening. Of all the wild animals and birds the Creator wanted me to be sedentary while you are one who travels about. Since the cock was successful and outstanding in his manly duties he has been given several beautiful brides[18] and that's why he was forbidden to walk out on them. After having this, what is it to go to Qof Mountain and look for Semurgh?'

LX

Hoopoe's Answer to the Rooster

Hoopoe answered:

'If a person says anything about their life, there is a reason behind it. Truly, there is a bird like this that has not opened his wings to fly but

---

[18] 'Hens.'

has a nest on the branches of the tree in Seventh Heaven. He makes that place his facility for seclusion, but wherever he wanders it will still be his homeland. Although he discretely flew to the throne of the highest heaven and sits on the tree he will not reveal his flying to people. Not one breath separates him from Semurgh. From the union in his heart another world radiates. His soul is not hurt by unrequited love because her form is always with him. The crown of charity glitters on his head as he himself does from the peak of love. He is satisfied with meeting her, but he cannot say anything and keeps his feelings hidden from others. Although, his heart is raging with union's one hundred thousand pearls, his mouth stays closed like a pearl shell.[19]

'You are not like a bird whose voice is displeasing. However, you are a speaker of all kinds of lying and illicit words. You lead an extremely depraved life day and night. You pass your time by meaningless cries and shouts, and by making your rounds amongst the females. You display a hundred kinds of evil and yet you compare yourself with good people. Today you advocated such lethargy. Hey hen, don't call yourself a rooster.'

LXI

The Birds Question Hoopoe About their Place with Semurgh

Every bird addressed Hoopooe with their excuses and he rebutted each with the necessary answers. The birds felt weak in contrast to his words and now had no inclination to employ other excuses.

Feeling poor before Hoopoe they asked:

'O bird whose kind is governance's pearl and whose head is worthy of the crown that shows the right way! You have traversed several deserts, and yet your resolve of the opportunity of the road has held fast. You know all the difficulties of this road and how to avoid its dangers.

'We, however, are a needy and weak flock. Since we are unfortunate our happiness has turned to misery. This secret is not light for our hearts, because our ignorance is more than more and our knowledge is less than

---

[19] Here Nava'i is referring to the principles of the Sufi order of Naqshbandi.

less. If Semurgh is a bright sun in the perfect sky we drift like a dust participle. Our situation is to be pitied. His place is higher than Heaven. His place reaches to the throne. It is as wide as the long distance of the road to Paradise! He is higher than nine heavens and we are less than one simple straw. What does his average comparison have to do with us? Is there wisdom in this comparison? If he is the king of the shahs' shah then we are the beggars' beggar who lie on the docile dirt of the road. These ideas are black to us. Inform us, as our intelligence is weak; let us be aware of these things that we are not able to conceive. We are pathetic and he is a person of high breed, now tell me, what is the difference between a drop of water and the sea?'

LXII

Hoopoe's Answer to the Birds and Semurgh's Visible Expression

Hoopoe gave his kin the following answer:
'Semurgh is like a noble shah. The preserver of the world's beauty that originally was a secret treasure. However, there was no mirror to reveal Semurgh's beauty. Trying to see himself he slowly began to radiate. While he was radiating like the sun a hundred thousand shadows were shown. The more the shadow gleamed the more it was noticed. The shadows of all the world's birds consist of his wisdom.

'Now you know this wisdom. That is the comparison between you and Semurgh. If you understand the meaning of it, O slow-witted sibling, don't disclose it to anyone else. He who discovers this secret will think long about it and if his mind becomes mature with truth he will surely say in shock, 'God save me!' If you meditate on the truth, what else is there to say except that the truth he is comprised of is oneness. In this case one needs to say that he has been entwined with truth.

'You ascertained whose shadow you were and what was your foundation. If Semurgh had not wanted to have his shadow and radiate he would not have been the shadow's owner. If Semurgh had wanted to conceal himself his shadow would not have been seen. However, since the shadow's revelation, the existence of the shadow's giver can be proven. If your eyes did not encircle Semurgh your heart would not be reflective as

a mirror. If you don't have those kinds of eyes it is impossible to see his face; there is no other way. He wanted lovers of his beauty. So he created a mirror like the sun to make his radiance and beauty visible and could know those who fell in love with his beauty. O people of the heart! This mirror is the soul, and it continually reflects God. His beauty's elegance has been revealed and with your heart you serve him as a mirror. Through your heart you can know him.'

LXIII

A Shah's Story of How He Demonstrated His Beauty Through a Mirror

There was a shah with a beautiful face like the full moon in the sky. All the moonlike beauties in the world were his servants, and he was their shah. Even the Cyprus and the Sun felt ashamed when they saw the shah's figure. The whole world knew about his charming face. Everybody tried to see and be in love with that heart-killing beauty. The world was enrapt in the shah's beauty and his love robbed everyone. The owner of the beauty who had given such beauty to the world also had coquetry, which was hundred times more than his beauty. If he came on horse to the square those that saw his beauty immediately surrendered their spirit. When he traveled the road it became crowded with people who then perished. Due to his beauty the world craved more and the possessions of their souls were plundered.

Innumerable people were wiped out because of its sentence. He dreamed of showing his beauty to the people. Therefore, by his order a mirror was made and it was installed in front of the throne. Also, a shining scene like a star that reflected the mirror was decorated beside the castle. When he looked into the mirror he would see his beauty and the people enjoyed it through the scene. Until that mirror had been made nobody could glance at his beauty and enjoy it. Having done this he could enjoy his beauty and the people looking for it could also enjoy it.

'Imagine this mirror as a soul that displays this beauty's reflection. Imagine the castle as a person's body and the mirror as his soul and see the shah's beauty in that mirror. The king will not look into that mirror until it gleams. You should know that his beauty is reflected in the

mirror and that you are standing in front of him taking it in. How clear the mirror is determines how perfect the reflection will be.'

LIV

Alexander the Great's Story about Being an Emissary

One day Alexander decided to appoint himself as an emissary. This work of Alexander resembles the dove, which had to take a message to Semurgh. The dove needed to accomplish his task and be the messenger of the shah's letter. Alexander came to the country, with an entourage, as an emissary should, and declared his message to the people who lived there with: 'These are the words of Alexander the Great.' Now this was interesting because he himself was Alexander the Great. He spoke for the entourage and informed the people of the declarations. How should they have known that he was Alexander? Everybody thought he was the courier of the empire's ruler. No one was aware of the edicts and the emissary's true mark and what he was up to. The people from a thousand to one did not know about this situation. No one perceived the design of this act or it's purpose.

'You also speak about the king and want to reach him. However, will it be achieved by reciting meaningless stories?'

In this way the birds discovered the figurative meaning in these words. Everyone understood how to reach their aim. Wanting these things, they revived their love once again. So, the leader Hoopoe spoke warmly and informed the others. Again all the birds addressed to him these questions:

'O owner of beauty in the house of rulers who is able to show the right way! We are a flock that is extremely needy and weak, our soul is feeble, our body is thin and frail. The task before us is huge and the road is long with many dangers and difficulties. How can we make it through?'

LXV

Hoopoe's Answer to the Birds' Question about the Road

Hoopoe gave his kin this answer:

'The right attitude is that on this road the highest virtue is love. People who are in love, however, are far from advising it. Whoever is in love is not afraid of their soul, can let go of their faith,[20] and is not reluctant to be a heretic. If the lover gets his beloved it will be easy for him to give up his soul and world. Like one who encounters a pit on his road, the soul is also an obstacle on the lover's road. The lover will be separated from body, soul, reason, consciousness, blasphemy, and faith.

'Love makes the world burn, and sets fire to the soul! His passion will burn blasphemy and faith. The one who loves does not care about shame and honor. Passion, being on fire, and illness are appropriate for love. It encompasses the world like lightning. For the one who is overcome by illness and love it is better to relinquish his soul for it. What does the one whose thoughts are on the beloved have to fear about the destruction of his soul? The work of love is to endure sorrowful nights, illness and to burn. Those rays of the world would serve him as a candle. Only from burning in love will this ailment make itself known. For if you are not the master of illness than it is impossible for the soul to be sacrificed.

'O singer, sing a sad song! O cupbearer, I am to be killed for my lack of illness. Make me miserable until love's illness affects my heart. Let me drink it and relinquish soul, reason, consciousness, religion, and faith! Let me inside the unbelievers' tavern, lie on the Christians' belt[21] and hang the icon. Let me become drunk in front of the tavern's elder, burn the Qu'ran and become an idol worshipper. In love's tavern let me free my soul from faith's shame. Let me listen to the bell's sound in the idol house. Let me kiss the ground to worship the idol. Let me firmly tie the Christians' belt and make the heretics happier than I.'

---

[20] This has to do with the mystic concept that the one who truly knows God and self does not need the mere forms and regulations of religion.

[21] 'Zunnor' – this is the belt that was worn by Christians and Jews to distinguish them from Muslims. It also implies a person that worships objects.

LXVI

A Story

Shaikh San'on[22] attained a station where his heart was aware of hidden secrets. In Ka'ba[23] he lived and among the saints and clan leaders was seen to be just like a prophet. He was the guide of the right way for the people and the Shaikh of all Shaikhs in Ka'ba. Shahs used to be beggars at his threshold and educated people were proud to praise him. If he wanted to bless a depressed person he would open angelic hands and say an 'Amen'. His purpose was to show the star to those in front of him, and his heart's mirror reflected much. People interjected their face in the midst of his path and would shine in the mirror of his soul. The number of his close followers was four hundred. Each of them was equal to Junaid[24] and Boyazid.[25] When he gave a blessing, even one who darkened the world with wretched smoke became lighter. If a person had any disease it would disappear after his praying. His splendor distressed the high sky and the high heaven seemed to be low before his generosity. The high heaven informed his knowledge, and like revelation or inspiration changed them into reality. If he saw something in his dream, this event from head to foot, would become true a hundred times.

For several nights he was forcibly shown a recurring dream. The dream picked apart his thread of patience and resolution. Awakening, he would repent of his state, if his eyes slumbered that dream would come again. In his dream he was walking along in some strange place. Then it became clear that it was Rome. He was standing drunk in an idol house and like the drunken people in that church he also belonged to idolatry.

---

[22] Shaikh Sanon (Ibn as-Saqo) was a man of eminence under the Caliphs of Baghdad during the eleventh and twelfth centuries. The true story of his passionate love for a Christian girl and the leaving of the Muslim faith was famous in many Eastern countries. Farididdin Attar was the first to describe this story in " *Mantiq-ut-tayr* " in 1221.

[23] This is the cube-shaped stone building in the center of the main Mosque in Mecca. It contains the black stone that was white when it had fallen from heaven, but has now become black because of the sins of those who have touched it.

[24] Junaid Baghdodi was a famous Shaikh. He died in 910.

[25] Boyazid Bistomi - his full name was Tayfun binni Iso binni Adam. He is the great Shaikh who founded the Tayfuriya order of Sufism. He died in 961.

After the dream had repeated many times, the Shaikh who was the treasurer of secrets said to his followers:

'It looks like I won't be freed of this trouble. If a person is in Ka'ba or in the church of fire worshippers,[26] then there is no way but to see what is written on the wall. I need to make my way to that country quickly and be taken to where my fate is. Let us go there and see what happens. Whatever comes upon our heads, we will say 'O destiny' when we see it.'

When he examined his state he found no other way but to go to that native land. Before leaving he touched the Ka'ba with his face to say farewell, and with a hundred anxieties walked around it. After uselessly walking around it with a thousand difficulties he set out towards the continent of Rome.

Once his friends heard about his situation they accompanied him on the journey. While Tariqat's[27] elder continued down the road four hundred people of the way accompanied him. On the way many problems troubled the Shaikh. Every time he was in difficulty he had no means to get rid of it. His friends were surprised at his state and their intellect could not make sense of it. His friends would ask him: 'What happened to you?' They did understand his strange situation. When they could not find the answer to their questions then they became more troubled than the Shaikh.

So, they went forward to the goal. What goal? Perhaps the goal of extreme strife. When he reached the native land his heart immediately began to encounter a hundred varieties of troubles.

Every time they walked along a strange idol house would suddenly appear. Its ceiling reached the dome of the sky and in it's ceiling many secrets had been concealed. The stones of this building were brought from the sad mountain and its bricks formed from the troubled earth. The bricks were finished by using a hundred steps, colorful paints, and by combining several beautiful designs. The schemes of the balcony made the people do stand and gawk, putting them into a helpless state, and there was no way to be free of it. Every opening of the building was lit with love's ray, but in these opening's various evils resided. The notches of the building tried to break through belief and reveal love's stain. Every stone of the cog looked like a head cut off by the blade of love. It was as if these stones

---

[26] Zoroastrians.
[27] The way of Sufism.

were created to make religious people's heads fly and for the setting off of rocks all over the world. The gate was the passage for conspiracy's group and the ceiling that was full of incitements took its pattern from the sky. The door loops and chains consisted of a hundred thousand tricks and encircled the group with worries' loop, and made them go crazy as senselessness' chain bound them.

There were one hundred pagan churches and inside them one hundred fire worshipers caught on fire with love's flame. Each church with black smoke coming from them covered the idol house's columns like the very darkness of blasphemers and rebellion. The ancient world with it's many rotations had not yet seen such an astonishing idol house.

When the Shaikh arrived his temperature went up and his heart began to be have unbearable anxiety. Every time sickness turned upon him another strange world began to appear before his eyes. While he wildly glanced in all directions, his eyes unwillingly came back to one direction. A beauty with a veil on her face appeared before him. This veil seemed to hide her sun-like face that resembled a rainbow on the horizon. At that moment the wind blew and raised her veil and the sun's rays began shining every direction. Do not call her the sun, perhaps a hundred suns were senseless before her like a moth around beauty's candle.

The figure and form of this beautiful girl were like a spirit in a picture and every moment a hundred postures were in the spirit. She was a charming virgin, and her crimson cheek was a pure Cyprus. Her glances charmed the spirit and the characteristic of her form could put a person into a hundred contortions. Angels and fairies felt embarrassed due to her picture, and the eastern sun was also made ashamed by her face. Her face scattered light and her hair was blacker than darkness. As if this light and darkness was the sign of blasphemy and belief. Her fragrant hair hung in curls down her face. As if in this darkness, light's concealment was recalled. Her hair appeared as darkness to people who where of light. It seemed that the lovesick people's great territory was hidden. Just like the new moon that surprised the mad man, so her eyebrows seemed to be like a new moon to the love-stricken ones. The ceiling of her eye-brows and the eyelids of her eyes were troublesome just like the beautiful girl who stood under the ceiling of that church. Surrounding her eyes were her eyelashes, which went in every direction in rows like plotters. There was a beauty mark under her two eyes that looked like a dot under the Arabic

letter 'b' in the word 'balo.'[28]

Her mouth gave a trace of hidden secrets, but one cannot see them since they belong to secret people. Her lips were salve for sick souls, in her speech was the animating breath of Jesus Christ. Her merry-making lips were red as a ruby. From her words sick souls received nourishment. In her laughter, hundreds of thousands of souls were captured by the pit of her dimple that could hold one hundred Josephs[29] captive. If she wanted to save those who had fallen in the pit she would toss her long hair, but even with this assistance more would be caught in her band. The circumference of her double chin looked like the dot of the Arabic letter 'nun'.[30] It was as if it served as a dome to life-giving water but it was not very high. When she walked her young figure illuminated life. Her eyes and lips displayed strange wonders, if one of them killed people, the second one brought those dead ones back to life.

Her body was a red flower, and the dress she wore was as a flower upon flower. The person who saw her would immediately have one hundred thousand agitated hearts and be lost. Her dress had color on color and beautiful decorations. One could observe the soul-bearing labor done by Roman and European experts. If the red color of the dress served to execute people the scent of her brought the dead people's soul back. Everybody wanted to enjoy the eyes, which slaughtered religious people as non-believers. Whoever thought of her hair to be a Christian belt found their religion and faith destroyed. Her beauty and charm was too pleasant among souls. Just a sip from her is like a mouthful of water. If her beauty's gleam made everything smolder, her flaming ruby made the soul burn. Possessors of intelligence and awareness found love from her flames and monks burned with her love and became ash.

In short, in that Christian girl's beautiful figure stood on top of the castle like Jesus' daughter on the terrace of the sun. The Shaikh felt exhaustion in his heart and his soul sank in the beauty's sea. He was very anxious and

---

[28] Denotes "evil" in Arabic and Uzbek.

[29] Joseph was thrown into a well by his envious brothers.

[30] This Arabic letter looks like the circumference of a double chin with a dot above it. This dot represents to Nava'i the deep pit of a beauty mark.

recited the prayer of peace.[31] Within it he said again and again 'repent'. He knew he was on the edge of being seized. However, she burnt down the Shaikh's repentance and prayers with the gleam of her beauty. The Shaikh was faint and about to fall to the ground. At that moment the staff in his hand buttressed his body just like a house's pillar. Then he leaned against a wall and was astonished by his unusual state. However, as his staff and body were badly damaged from his heart-racing anxiety he still fell down weak.

Therefore, his pure soul fell in love. It entered him like blood and spread all over his body. He was sometimes faint and sometimes conscious. His companions were speechless in regards to his state. They looked at each other in shock. Seeing the Shaikh's condition they either hung their heads or hopelessly clapped at him. At nightfall his state remained and he experienced further trauma and he wandered about.

The country of night made the day dark and around that idol house blasphemies' gloom covered everything like darkness. Like dark destiny night fell upon his head. In the same way his household was subject to the same dark misfortune. All of them remained on the ground of the Zoroastrian idol house. Which ground? Better perhaps to say the mountain of evil. The Shaikh's head experienced great heaviness. No human has seen such a dark night like this.

The curtains of ill fortune were spread out in the night sky and on every side the nails from the stars were hammered. Smoke caused the eye of the sky to shed its tears. Around the sky it became chaotic. The sky stopped rotating and like a mountain did not sway from its place. The sky oppressed ailing people and created a tremendous amount of sorrows. The world disappeared in those mountains and one hundred thousands stones were poured down. The sky scattered stars from its eyes and made known it's sign of mourning over the Shaikh's state. The people of the world mourned and wore black clothes.

The Shaikh's head had never experienced such difficulties like these and he was extremely depressed and weak. Due to tyranny's love, in his weakness he became ill. In a state of misery and desperation he lay down on the idol house's ground. Love lit his body and soul and put his blasphemy,

---

[31] 'Lohavl.'

religion, and faith on fire. Having lied down his tears poured forth, but with every breath his mouth became dry as the fire in his heart was flaming out of his mouth. If love scorched his house then night scorched his sleep.

He was destitute due to the hundreds of misfortunes of his destiny. Crying over it, he lamented:

'With every breath my sorrows increase. O heavens, what are you doing to me? You shattered my peace, dragged me towards love, and threw me into a hundred fires. First you let the bright sun enter my soul, and then you hid it and confined me to the darkness of sorrow's evening. Not only have you darkened sorrow's evening but also the span of the sky. The smoke from sorrow's hell covers the earth as it arises from the flame you alit in my soul.

'Allah! Allah! What kind of night is this? How can one have such a cruel night? I have had a lot of hard nights, but I have never experienced such a sorrowful night. Perhaps this darkness is not night, but rather the smoke of hell's fire. Or is it the essence of heaven's sighs? O Lord, no one should have to experience a night like this.

'I do not know if I should speak about my night's troubles or about my day's misfortunes? My body, emotion, reason, and consciousness are veiled in love. Hidden as if none of them exist. It appears as if they have all been destroyed under the yoke of love. Neither health nor patience remains within my body. Therefore, like the way of tears, the strength to move on cannot be found.

'Where can I find the strength to smash my head on the stone in order to end this limitless distress and sorrow? Where are the eyes with which to look upon the girl with the face as beautiful and radiant as the moon and find joy in her radiant light? Where is a face that will grovel in the dirt like the slave who pleads before a shah? Where are the hands that will pick up stones to beat my chest and pour dirt on my head? Where is the consciousness that opposes the taking of my hand and it being led away to a place where I will go crazy? Where is the reason to plan a course of action for love and the restoration of a ruined heart? Where is the patience, to cure my sickness and remove the distress from my heart? Where is the soul to care for the wounds of my sorrow? It is counted as dead now. Again, where is the heart that will beat even for a moment? Just as the soul, I cannot find it.

'Was this way not the way of disaster for me? Truly, it could not be

worse. Wouldn't it be better for me to die than lead a sorrowful life like this? I wish lightning would strike and leave no trace of me!

'O friends, what would have happened to you if you had assisted me? What would have happened if you got together and had killed me in my desperation? Let the world be free of my shame and mourning. Brothers, stab my heart. Burn me and pour my ashes out over the land. Do not let such dishonor as this remain in world. Let me die once rather than die one hundred times in every moment.'

The Shaikh's friends were taken aback by his tragic state, and they bitterly wept over his illness. They gathered in sorrow and pity and began giving the Shaikh various words of advice. The Shaikh could not understand their counsel or the purpose of their tender words. If they appealed to the Shaikh with reasonable arguments the Shaikh would rejoin with a love-smitten answer.

One of them said: 'O leader of the religious authorities! Your footprints can serve as mascara for those who follow you. Many people face this kind of temptation, but only one who is strong-willed can overcome.'

The Shaikh replied: 'What naivety! Even if I were one whose will was strong. I would still be unable to overcome.'

Another said: 'This is Satan's doing. If you do the ritual dances like him you will be able to get rid of him.'

The Shaikh replied: 'In that case you should all get together. But as for me I am one who has lost my senses. What help does that give me?'

Another said: 'O leader of the people who know secrets! In order to resist this evil you should say your prayers.'

The Shaikh said: 'Don't speak sense to me! I'm a mad-man and mad people are not instructed by reason.'

Another said: 'Stand up, do your ablutions and give the sign for the people to pray.'

The Shaikh reporter: 'I have no water except my tears and they are the blood that comes from my heart.'

Another said: 'You should do the observance and wash all the parts of your body since it purifies the soul and dispels sorrow. This is the best way!'

The Shaikh said: 'I drowned in the waters of nothingness. What else do you want of me?'

Another said: 'Guide your mind with the aid of a rosary and you will

find freedom from this state of senselessness.'

The Shaikh said: 'The thread of my rosary is broken and instead of it I have tied on the Christian cord.'

Another said: 'Ask for a toothbrush and once you have put it to your mouth, complete your prayers!'

The Shaikh spoke: 'If I wish to have a toothbrush in my mouth there is a finger of surprise waiting there for me.'

Another said: 'If you made a mistake than for you pardon kiss the ground in worship.'

The Shaikh shedding his tears of blood said: 'I cannot take my head from this doorway.'

Another said: 'You have gone to Rome, but now you need to make Ka'ba your home.'

The Shaikh said: 'What I was seeking there I have found here. Now, why should I go back and encounter extreme troubles.'

Another said: 'It is time to face the desert and head towards Mecca.'

The Shaikh said: 'I have found the holy place here. What am I to do with Mecca when I have Rome?'

Another said: 'Our journey is finished. It would be better if you came with us and returned to our homeland.'

The Shaikh said: 'The good Lord, showing compassion, provided this idol-house as my true homeland.'

Another said: 'You know that if the other Shaikhs find out about this they will blame us.'

The Shaikh replied: 'They are not my concern. The only person that I care for is in this tavern.'

Another said: 'Where is your formerly steadfast belief? What has happened to your old pure habits of religious zeal and diligent prayer?'

The Shaikh answered: 'I live to remain at the idol-house. I offer up one hundred of my former prayers for this.'

That night his clan was quite perturbed regarding their Shaikh's state. They considered reproaching the Shaikh, but they realized that he would pay them no heed. They gave advice, but he could not understand them. They lamented till morning and the idol worshippers watched their behavior. As the idol worshipers watched this clan, they began to mock their religious customs and rituals by throwing mud at them and boasting

about the superiority of their religion. The strayed ones considered 'lo'[32] in their word 'Lot'[33] to be equal to the 'lo' of the word 'illalloh'.[34] It was one thing for these people to be acquainted with unhappiness; it was yet another thing for the idol worshippers to now delight in their sorrows. Therefore, some of the Shaikh's close friends were converted, leaving the more religious ones disconcerted. The Muslims suffered greatly from this terrible situation until the light of morning shone forth.

As light overtook darkness the idolaters rang their massive bell. The spherical sun came into view and spread its rays like the display of a Christian girl's face. Amongst the idol worshippers the crisis of the Shaikh's love and trying circumstance became visible again. They gathered in the idol-house to seek comfort and the clergy rejoiced over this. The religious people were so ashamed that, finally, they could not endure the defamation any longer and they dispersed, leaving the Shaikh alone. Even the children of the church mocked the pitiful Shaikh and they enjoyed laughing over his state.

The old Shaikh was lying in the passageway, staring in the direction of the Christian girl. It was clear that he was both in love and quite miserable. He paid no attention to people even though they insulted, mocked, and abused him. Seeing the extent of his suffering, believers and non-believers alike felt sorry for him.

However, the one who made the Shaikh's daylight into night called him from religion's road to be shamed in the non-believers idol-house. As he sought her, she hid behind a curtain, watching him all the while, she who set his world on fire. She remained ignorant – pretending not to know, not even trying to comprehend – that the Shaikh was ruined. She gave him no help. Although she vanquished his religion, she continued to ravage his soul, pretending all the while to be ignorant.

The Shaikh was in agony as a result of the separation from her. Whether he was in her presence or not he burned with lust. From early till late his heart broke; from night till dawn he was on the edge of death because of this separation. With every breath his torture seemed to increase and this state of affairs continued for a month. He faced exceeding sorrows and

---

[32] An Arabic letter.

[33] 'Idol.'

[34] 'Allah is one' is a sura from the Qur'an that is often said by Muslims.

maladies. In the midst of these sorrows the little remaining pride of his name nearly became equal to the dirt of the ground.

Finally, that cruel unbeliever and luring beauty was again seen at his place. The one, who had set his whole world ablaze and the initiated the affliction of his life, wanted to know more, and so with lovely coquetry presented this question:

'O leader of Islam's people, and the elder who shows the right way for the people of religion and Islam! It used to be your profession to walk around the Ka'ba. So, why did you make the door of an idol-house your home? They say you were the helper of religion's people, why then are you prisoner of the non-believers church? If people who travel spend a night here, the next day they continue on to another place, but you have been here for one month. You have made the ground of the idol-house your abode. You stayed at the church for one month and made it your abode. What do you hope to gain from living in the non-believers' church? What do you hope to obtain from the people of darkness?'

Having seen this beauty, who could decorate the world, and listening to her spirit-refreshing words his whole body trembled with excitement. Sometimes the members of his body were bent and sometimes they were straight. He lost consciousness and there was no sign of life in his body. The people in the idol-house suspected that he was dead and considered him to be as one who had already passed away a thousand years ago.

Day and night the Shaikh lay like a corpse. Seeing his state, the ideal beauty shook her head, and other non-believers were surprised and did not know what to say. Even the executioner felt sorry for him. Non-believers and believers gathered around his head and praised his perfect love. Yet, when they raised his head from the ground there still was soul in his body.

The Shaikh's love touched the hearts of the people and the idol beauty's heart was a hundred times changed. This girl, whose attraction caused the Shaikh's deathlike state came near to him. Smelling her scent he tried to slowly open his eyes to see the beauty. There was neither color in his face nor a word in his mouth. At that time he was as still as death and too weak to speak. Then the delight of being in her presence revived him. The despotic unbeliever put forth this request:

'We asked the Shaikh about his state to learn about his disposition.

However, the Shaikh pretended to be unconscious and did not open his mouth to tell us anything. Now he has returned and should answer our question.'

Having heard these words, the Shaikh sighed, tears poured forth from his eyes and he said:

'O one that has brought the Day of Judgment to my soul! Since you inquire after my state I have no other response but pleadings. Does it work to combine my pleas with hardship? For this way is no longer a mysterious secret and now having swallowed my malady I will not keep it from you any longer. In the idol-house I became weak and enslaved, bound with love's chain, and all kinds of torments accosted my soul. The reason for it all is the hope of seeing your face. What a wonderful place it is where the radiance of your face shines! It is like the shining of the sun from the fourth heaven; and it leaves me with neither patience nor endurance, emptying me of both reason and consciousness.

'Now I have told you in brief about myself and have made you aware of my malady. If you want to really understand it will be easy for you, but even if you kill me, my heart's love will live on. I have spoken this plea to you in order to gain your understanding. For it is up to you whether I die or receive mercy.'

The cruel girl then said to him:

'O guide endowed with noble qualities! I've heard that there is no shame among Muslims. So then isn't it strange that a leader of Muslims like yourself should speak such incoherent words? You have neither modesty nor etiquette. You seem to be eccentric and your words even more peculiar than yourself.

'O leader! You should know that whoever is in love should be only courteous and modest. O elder of the road! Even young children are not so audacious as to say these things that you have said. People are to call you 'Shaikh' aren't they? Are you not bringing shame to your white beard?[35] You are between ninety and a hundred, yet it is possible to say that you are both old and young. If you are young then your wisdom has yet to come and if you are old then it is not fitting for someone facing death to say such words. In light of your actions I am astonished to find that

---

[35] White beards are still a sign of a wise man in Central Asia.

you are so old, senile, and hunch-backed – you are not young at all! You have said many stupid things that no sensible person would say, although perhaps you could hear them from the mouth of a demon.

'O divided Shaikh! The words of your speech are not one with your heart. People in love keep their secrets hidden and are careful not to let them become exposed. Is it acceptable to share words like these hurriedly, especially before one's sweetheart? Do all people who fall in love do this? Is this an indication of the forbearance of the religious?'

Having heard the words of the beauty with a face like the moon, the Shaikh in his shame did not know what to do. The poor Shaikh felt very awkward and said to her:

'O you who capture all the beauty of humanity! Love made me frail and powerless, looted my reason and left me mad. Do you think people will expect wisdom from a madman? Or demand courteousness from a man who is senseless and bewitched? If I said anything abnormal because of my discourteousness, forgive me; I was not myself. However, all that I have said is true. If you do not believe me, you may check it. While my handsome body is in need and my soul is shattered, how can I speak a polite word to you? I suffer greatly, so please give me an answer? When you questioned me I was confused and so my answer was accordingly jumbled. To hide anything will not do, therefore I have told all of it. I cannot deny that I am under a trance and long to join my beloved.'

Therefore, the Shaikh did not take back what he had said, nor did he ask for her pardon. At this, the impishly obstinate girl retorted:

'O malicious man! If you agree with destiny, then whoever would like to reach me must meet my four conditions: he must drink, and then, being drunk, should tie on the Christian cord, burn the Qur'an in the fire, and adopt the idolatress' religion.

'These four conditions are the requirement for my love, its offering. In addition, it has two penalties. For there are four ways to nothingness and two more ways of overcoming these four. One way is to breed swine for a year, and the second is during this period to tend the fire, making sure it remains lit in the idol-house.

'If the Shaikh has truly fallen in love with this idol-house beauty he can demonstrate his love's devotion by observing this offering and penalty. Can there be more misfortune than this? If you desire to join me and want

me to be by your side, you will have to accept all that I have said. Only then can you move to union with me. If your strength is not enough to do this, then change your course early in the day rather than late.'

The Shaikh said to her:

'O torturer of my ailing heart! I am suffering from your love's consuming fire. The passion you arouse in me is my torture. The ray of your passion envelops my entire existence and the lightning of your love scorches me. I am destitute and estranged— an alien to reason, awareness, and patience. For whatever the fairy-like darling commands there is no hesitation with this strange love. Whatever you demand or order, I obey, for you are my ruler. If I do not fulfill it, then slash my neck with torture's blade.'

The Shaikh's speech ended with this. The wicked girl and all the people of the idol-house were pleased with his words. Then the inside of the church was made like heaven as they took great pains to decorate it. A high throne, on a level with the sky was erected in the place of honor. It was adorned with an unbelievable quantity of precious stones and was incomparably beautiful.

The immoral Christian girl came to him, filled with fervor, and the Shaikh, having seen her, was close to dying. The Shaikh was placed in the midst of the crowd in order to besmear the face of his faith. Whether the idolaters lived there or had to travel from afar they were all present. They presented dozens of wine jugs and prepared various appetizers for later. The church bell and organs played to bid farewell to the Shaikh's religion.

Nothing like this had ever happened. The clergy representatives sat in a row; the presiding leader asked for the Qur'an and brought fire from the bonfire. When they brought a Christian cord and a cross the heart-comforting Christian girl stood up in sympathy. With sensual steps she descended the throne and proudly walked before the Shaikh. She sat beside him and drank a full goblet of wine. The cup-bearer refilled the goblet to the brim and she offered it to the Shaikh, saying:

'Drink till the bottom, O noble man! If one drop remains it will not be valid.'

With that the Shaikh, who was under the influence of love, began drinking gluttonously. With the tears that flowed from his eyes he washed his hands of Islam and faith completely. He drank so much that his head

felt filled with smoke and in the wine's fire his body became ash.

After the Shaikh drank wine for some time his love began afflicting his reason. When he became drunk and senseless he described his desire to be with the girl.

The cruel Christian girl, however, said to him, 'Only the first requirement has been fulfilled'.

The Shaikh said to her: 'What else must I do? Please tell me. Let me do whatever is necessary.'

Then the moon-like beauty gestured to the ones in authority, all of whom were masters in their fields. She presented the Shaikh's faith to the unbelievers and they adopted him into their religion. The tattered garb of his former position was removed and they undressed him. Whoever observed this event was sure to weep. Then he was placed in a pool of wine, wherein they bathed him. The Shaikh did not fear anything and continued plunging into the wine.

Then they brought clothes worn by unbelievers and dressed him with these from head to foot. They tightened the Christian cord around his waist and the Sufi leader became an unbeliever. Later they took the burdened Shaikh, who was wasting away, to the idol-house. In his drunken state, he worshiped in front of the idol, burned the tattered remains of his old robes of authority and flung the Qur'an into the fire. Having done this, one goblet after another was placed in his hands to send him off. In all these things he behaved like an idolater. He took part in every possible evil that the world afforded; not one bad thing remained inexperienced to him.

Love solved the difficulty of Ka'ba's secret in this way. He became the object of mockery for the children in the idol-house. Young gays from Europe in jest played with the drunken religious leader; he did not know what was going on around him and whenever he regained consciousness more wine was forced upon him. Utterly drunk, he lay either unconscious or in a state of stupor day and was oblivious to time.

Once again his heart overflowed with love. Early one morning he got up and noisily lamented:

'O torturer of my soul and destroyer my body! O creator of injustice and demolisher of my religion! Is this how the religion of unbelievers is? Is this the result of one of your requirements? Is this the reward of one's aims? Is this how you fulfill this kind of promise? Whatever your heart desired I did, but then a hundred thousand evil lightning bolts struck me. Now tell me please which of your duties did I not fulfill? Which of your

requirements did I not accomplish? When the time of keeping promises arrived, you stayed still as if you were ignorant. You did not keep your promise to join with me. I am poor, old, weak, and firmly tied with this unbelievers' chain. You shoved wine into my hands day and night and forgot about your promise. Is this the way you plan to prove your avowals? Are you not afraid now to pray to Manot and Lot?'[36]

The immoral Christian girl answered:

'O Shaikh! Stop criticizing me so much! Just as you tied the Christian cord around your waist, you fastened the requirements about you in consent, and therefore must complete them in their entirety. When you have fulfilled the four tasks, it will be the gift presented at our wedding! Now the two penalties of love remain. O great dignitary, the penalties consist of the following: without loathing you will burn a fire around the church the duration of each night for exactly one year. During the day despite your weakness you will set off for the swineherds and there till evening you will fill the role of shepherd for those animals.

'After the year is finished, come to meet me. Then I will prepare the feast of enjoinment; I will come to you and begin the wedding in the fashion of unbelievers and I will make your heart happy.

'If you are not ready to follow the regulations of love, don't continue this road. That is, if you do not fulfill the penalties as stated, then quit unbelief, accept your religion, leave the church, and go back to Ka'ba. Yet how many days did you drink continuously? I had devoted myself to your drinking of wine. Reject your old clothes that were burnt and don't speak again about their quality. If you demand a certain price for your clothes, alright take the money. And suspect that you have not seen anything yet and consider that your horse has yet to gallop towards the tavern of merry-making.'

Hearing the moon-like beauty's words, love wrung his heart again and he cried:

'O the vehemence of the ardor that is in my heart, the peace and power of my soul! Whatever you are, I am your slave ready to serve. If I do not fulfill it, fine, sentence me to death. But do not speak of separation and do not say a word about me having to leave the house of union.'

---

[36] The names of pre-Islamic Arab idols.

Then he jumped up from his seat and said:

'Bring the flock of swine. Amass them before their shepherd! Be considerate and help me, the lost one, and lead me towards the place of fire.'

So, a flock of swine was brought into his presence and his second wish was fulfilled. In the daytime the Shaikh watched the flock of swine and during the nights he kindled the fires.

From evening to dawn he had to keep the fires lit. He spent his time kindling the unbelievers' fire, making it ever brighter. In the early morning when the church bells tolled, that is after the dark night became lighter, he would come out of the ashes, completely covered in soot, looking like a mad man who had fallen into a fire. In addition, like a Christian, he tried to hum the music of the bell as he stood under it. In this manner, he was face to face with pigs, more than a hundred around him.

'Therefore, the Shaikh remained as a captive, afflicted with this darkness. The people previously under his rule tried numerous measures in hopes of freeing him, but their measures were in vain. Finally, when they could not find a way to free him, out of despair they dispersed, leaving the Shaikh on his own. They all left accompanied by shame, and like fugitives sought refuge in the Ka'ba.

The Shaikh once had a pupil marked by self-abandonment, who drank an immoderate amount of wine from the bowl of love. Wherever the company of the Shaikh would move, his pupil would accompany him. However, when the Shaikh went to Rome, his student had been somewhere else. When this propitious traveler returned from his journey he passed by many pilgrimage stops on his way to Ka'ba. Even on the way the pupil wanted to find shelter near the Shaikh, and so he set out for the meetinghouse. When he arrived at the meetinghouse he discovered that the Shaikh was in dire straits and that his former teacher was no longer there, but was taken over by a poor Shaikh. Also, none of the four hundred religious people of the meetinghouse were to be seen. Once he examined the case thoroughly he was told everything that had occurred. He heard the recount of the Shaikh's journey to Rome and the crisis' that had come upon him there.

Since he was the caliph of the Shaikh's pupils he sent messengers to gather his colleagues. He showed them grace, assembled them and attentively inquired about the Shaikh's circumstances. He was informed about the dream, the events in Rome, the idol-house, and the Christian girl's cruelty. They told him the story of the Shaikh's drinking of love and consequent weakness, his state of acquiescence, his drinking wine and becoming rough and drunk, his abandoning the faith and becoming an idolater, his work of fire kindling, his putting God's Word into the fire, his wrapping the Christian cord around his torso four times, and how he even now lights the fires at the fire house during the night and tends swine during the day.

With this the master of sickness who enlightened wine lovers said to the people:

'O people whose preserving modesty and honor is worse than pigs! The Shaikh was your elder and you were his disciples. Everybody found contentment and hope from his instruction. The requirements of poverty and discipleship are these: whoever is gracious and a guide in spiritual matters, then his disciples will likewise be like him. Whether the day is good or bad you should mimic what is done. Shame on you for your customs of impoverishment and disloyalty! Shame on you for wearing Sufi clothes and turbans!

'When everything is good, out of your deceptiveness, you try to cheat and prove your loyalty to the Shaikh. Yet, when the Shaikh encountered some problems you pulled far away from him. You were untrue and left your Shaikh in the church. When this problem fell upon his head, you did not fear God, and were not ashamed of our nation, you left him alone and turned back. Tired of serving and seeing your leader, you left him there. With such qualities you considered your ideas as good, and called each other 'dervish',[37] as ones who do right deeds. Shame on you for your religious garb; for your Islamic footwear, turban and staff! If the Shaikh had bred dogs, perhaps some would have been loyal and a balm for his difficulties. Even if some of them went away, surely a few would stay and not move from his side. They would growl at his antagonists and lift their voices in grief if he died. If a person is far from being loyal then it would be better to have a dog that is loyal. And if you had bravery it would be required for you to also be loyal to your Shaikh when these hard times came upon

---

[37] The title for an experienced Sufi. They often belong to a Shaikh and his order of dervishes.

his head, particularly when he became smitten with love and did not know what to do. However, you were far from sympathizing with him, and in this your cowardliness was revealed. If a man exaggerates that he is a man can he be a man? Can he do what he is incapable of doing?'

The faithful pupil was speaking soul-nourishing words like these while the other disciples sat silently, not saying a word. After he scolded them he stood up saying: 'The work will not be finished by sitting here.' This animator of religion and faith started off for Rome, towards the place that would illuminate his religion and belief. Supporting him completely, that crowd became his fervent followers. They passed through the wastelands and came across the shepherd of swine. There was not a trace of Islam or faith in him, nor any sign of reason, religiosity, righteousness or meekness.[38] This senseless lover, drunk on wine, was sick of achieving nothing.

The Shaikh did not recognize the people who had come to him and turned his face away from them in the direction of the wandering swineherd.

Seeing this situation, the aspiring Sufis pitied the Shaikh and sighed. He whose eyes had torrents of sorrowful tears faced the crowd who had come with him and said:

'Now praise God, don't loiter here, come back with us! The eyes of our master of perfection and elder have grown dim with love's mayhem.'

The faithful pupil then returned to the city, found the head of the fire worshippers and stated his purpose to the people of this world of oppression. Then in the presence of the true beloved he began crying beseeching tears day and night. His mission was to liberate the Shaikh, to pray and beg his pardon. He was loyal to his purpose and he belonged to loyal people. With much striving he prayed a lot and finally God accepted his prayer.

One night his tears of pleading flowed, and from this intense weeping he became ill. At dawn his eyes closed for one moment. Then he dreamed of marvelous rays emanating from a shining sun behind it. That sun was so big that one hundred minor suns could fit in it. It was the last messenger of the prophet-hood and was the best of Hoshim's[39] lineage, his stamp and ring. He came smiling and his life-giving lips were inclined to speak. When the treasure of secrets appeared the faithful pupil prostrated himself

---

[38] Muslim attributes are implied here.
[39] Muhammad's great-grandfather.

before him and began pleading that he would hear his needs.

'O one who honorably provides for the ill, the owner of the prophets' throne! There is no need to speak about my situation, because everything is clear in the illumination of your heart.'

The shah of prophets spoke with the honor of one thousand men:

'O one who is an open flower in the garden of your hope! I salute you in your honorable plan springing from your loyalty! Your pleading was so woeful that God, who orders things well, has seen your weakness and listened to your entreaties. Aware of your groans and pains he has conceded to answer your prayers. Only by overcoming the obstacles that God erects may one have entrance into the way of his secret wisdom; it is impossible to find help without overcoming these impediments. Your Shaikh has crossed one such potent test. No other traveler has ever had such a situation as he. God, in his generosity, gave aid and this pleased him. Give thanks and rid yourself of grief. Indeed, you have seen many difficulties, but because of you, God has shown mercy to your elder.'

When Allah's prophet shared these secrets with the faithful disciple, tears of joy ran down from the eyes of the entreater. In his happiness he let out one sigh and then lost consciousness, falling down due to his extreme weakness.

The morning breeze began blowing, filled with the scent of musk. Then the night's scent retreated and the day came. The weak disciple, now revitalized, jumped to his feet. He then bowed low in the place where he had been standing and pleading with God, since in truth God's duty had been fulfilled. The friends who were with him questioned him, and after they heard a full account, they all accompanied him on his way. As the wind that dishevels the surface of grass or stirs the top of water, they went in the direction of the Shaikh with their hearts bewildered. Sometimes they passed over the highlands and sometimes the lowlands until they came to the place where the love-smitten Shaikh resided.

The Shaikh was loosed from deviation as the awareness of his lifelessness overtook him. A breeze from the garden of assistance touched his heart and tears of shame were seen in his eyes and he suffered the pain of regret. He cast off the clothes of the unbelievers as well as the Christian cord. His heart, which had been harmed by blasphemy was pierced by a ray of the light that illumines the right way.

At that moment the followers arrived. When they came the Shaikh felt

proud. Likewise, when they saw the Shaikh's state it produced changes in them and they gave a hundred thanks for this. They rejoiced and said:

'O elder who was in love! The good news for you is that Muhammad has helped you.'

The Shaikh was aware of what had happened. He told his group about it and tightly hugged his faithful and wise pupil to his chest. The Shaikh said to him:

'O my blessed son, the bond of my heart. In your display of fidelity you did not waver or show any deficiency in friendship. With what language must I beg your forgiveness? May God himself pardon your fidelity!'

His pupil also shed tears of joy and did not raise his head from his elder's feet. Overcome with emotion at the sight of the two, no one knew what to do until the two calmed down.

His supporters said:

'O leader! God destined this country to us. Now it is time to leave this dangerous place and go in the direction of Ka'ba.'

The Shaikh washed himself and put on the customary Muslim clothes. Those who saw it were filled with happiness. Passing through the wasteland, they set out for Ka'ba with zeal. They said that the Shaikh should continue on his way to Ka'ba, but that they should go back to the Christian girl. The fairy was fast asleep. She saw a dream in which the Eastern sun descended in the sky and the following news was brought to that cruel girl from the prophet Jesus:

'O one who is immature in the realm of loyalty! The elder of this period, Shaikh Sanon, came to your idol-house as a guest. However, you did not uphold the tradition of hostess. Why did you torture his days? He has now abandoned the hospitality of the idol-house and has started on his way to Ka'ba where he will be a host. Go to him, adopt his religion, ask his forgiveness and be his spouse.'

The Christian girl woke from her slumber hoping to see the Shaikh's footprints. Remembering all that she had done, her dejected heart became depressed. She arose with a sigh and began her journey to Ka'ba. Tears were falling from her eyes like the stars in the sky and she was weeping like Majnun's beloved Laili.[40] Her departure in the direction of the Shaikh

---

[40] This is a famous couple in Persian literature. They represent dear but hard love, somewhat like Romeo and Juliet. Nava'i has written his own epic poem on the couple. For a long time Majnun had to love Laili from distance but one day that changed.

and his people was hurried, like a petal of a new flower blown by the wind. As she was walking the heavens took revenge for what she had done and so she became extremely weak. The vehement malice and animosity of the heavens increased in the wasteland and the girl began to experience anxiety and fear. In the seemingly endless wasteland, nausea and weakness confronted her.

She said:

'O my Lord! I am weak and dizzy and have shed the blood of my eyes and soul. Have mercy in my desperation! Have mercy for I am alone! Although I have nothing but sins and guilt I have no one else but you to protect me.'

She wept bitterly since she was all alone without any help. Punishment displayed its power to the beauty so that she was weakened and fell face down to the ground. When she fell down she lost consciousness. There she lay neglected and sick.

The high ranking Shaikh was aware of what was happening. The miracle-worker accompanying the Shaikh was also aware of an amazing sign.

His moon-face beauty, his weak and sorrowful beauty, was face to face with that miraculous sign as well. At that time that strong wine-lover who was traveling far away from her, suddenly turned back. All the people that were accompanying the Shaikh also quickly turned back, although they were unaware of his thoughts. They thought: 'O Lord, what is the reason for turning back?'

The Shaikh and his confidants reached the place where the beauty was lying. Despite the Shaikh's full comprehension of what happened he could do nothing but weep. He immediately placed the head of the unconscious girl on his bosom. Tears began dripping from the Shaikh's eyelashes onto the girl's face. As this dew sprinkled onto the flower's petals, the wilted sleeping flower seemed to bloom. When the girl realized that her head was on the Shaikh's bosom, tears of sorrow began pouring down her face.

Since she was weak her groans were not audible and drops of blood flowed out of her heart and washed her face.

Then the girl said to the Shaikh:

'O one whose watchword has been religiosity and whose shelter has been religion! Which language can I use to ask for your forgiveness? Rebellious and pitiful children threw stones at a tall tree that provided

them shade. But even if a hundred thousand rose bush thorns raise their heads, each of them will blossom because of the spring clouds. Although my sin is great I hope that the mercy that is in you is greater. Knowing my crassness I come before you with a dirty face, desiring your forgiveness. Whatever evil I did before was due to my own evil, and the evil of my homeland and religion. I have many more secrets and they are in a rush to be told, but we have very little time left.'

She then made her interest in Islam known and one by one explained the signs that Jesus had spoken of. At last she said:

'I will stop my abrupt speech here. I come to faith, hurry, I have very little time.'

Then tears flowed from the Shaikh's face and he pleaded for the faith of his Christian soul mate. When the girl came to faith in secret, she took one last deep breath and died[41] before the Shaikh. Then the religious people began to wail and grieve. An unusual thing happened, this caused there to be mutual understanding between the two religions.

'Marvels like this and other interesting events are not rare among those who are in love. These marvels can reveal new tricks. Love is a sea that has no limit. Each bubble in the sea points to the limitless sky. Love is a world and it is very wide. Love is a sky and it is very high. Here, the dimmest star called 'Suho' can overturn the heavens, and a fly can weaken the legendary bird called Anqo[42]. If a spark from love reaches it, than its damage will be greater than a hundred lightning bolts. Every drop in this sea can destroy the surface of the world by its evil muddy tributaries. If the blade of love is revealed to have slaughtered one hundred thousand people, in its presence taking revenge or blood money will be useless. A person who has had suffered much at the hands of love will only be satisfied by being ready to take their own life.

'How striking that in the garden of love one's very vision is altered, the clarity of the water and the vibrant hues of the rainbow are as startlingly pure as the blood of sinless people. Every eyelash of your beloved seems to be strung with hundreds of thousands hearts, such is the magnified impact of every detail of her beauty. It is like a beauty mark that blinds one hundred

---

[41] Literally, 'her soul was found.'
[42] See footnote three above.

thousand eyes.[43] In the country of love a poor man and a shah are one; in the tavern a guide and the lost are considered equal. And in love there is nothing but illness, misfortune, weakness, and constant torment.

'The Shaikh fell in love to such an extreme extent that his disgrace spread the world over. Its clamor was so great that it also threatened the possession of my heart. If a person is in such a state as I, it does not mean that his is better or worse off. Come Nava'i, let your words stop here; don't speak more about love and the many cures. If I come across a peaceful day in my life, I want sit down and write an explanation of my love in the form of an epic poem. Then an honest person will be able to distinguish whether what I have said is true or an exaggeration.'

'In conclusion, after the Shaikh suffered from the pain of separation and completed his work at the idol-house, he prepared to go to Ka'ba. He buried his soul mate in a tomb at the graveyard of the faithful and religious. In the same manner he had set out from Ka'ba to the idol-house he returned from the idol-house to Ka'ba. He asked and begged God's pardon for his past deeds and at last his confession was accepted and he joined his soul mate in paradise.'

LXVII

Lots were Cast and Hoopoe was Chosen as Leader of the Flock

Having heard these astounding words, the birds' consciences were elevated to a higher plane and they no longer fretted over their everyday problems. Love took possession of their will and they became wary of their fleeting desires. With lightning-speed, they covered the road. To go from the West to the East was nothing for them. They were in a hurry as they faced new grades of danger with every breath they took. Some of them were able to traverse the long road, but others were unable to due to their weakness. These would then become separated from the flock and rest where they were. Then finding themselves lost, they would haphazardly

---

[43] In Arabic script if the dot (represented here by the 'beauty mark') in the word 'eye' were taken away, the meaning would change to 'blind'. In this sentence 'love is blind' or 'love makes the eye blind' is implied.

head out in various directions.

It was clear that a guide was necessary among the flock. The guide would watch over them. For, without leadership, chaos would emerge, its effects throwing everyone into further confusion. If a shepherd does not direct his numerous sheep to grass and water, you can assume they will soon perish. Communities without leaders cannot move forward, for they do not know which way to go.

Since the journey ahead was very long and difficult, the birds unanimously decided:

'We need a wise and observant leader. Let him be the head of all birds. For we are feeble and the journey is very difficult. The flock needs a leader who would be both a guide and a companion.'

The birds, of high and low rank, that had started the journey unanimously chose Hoopoe for the job. They tried to persuade Hoopoe to accept the responsibility, but cautious about taking on the role of leader he stated:

'Yes, I should lead the flock as far as I am able. If you had another invitation I would accept it, but I cannot accept this job. For, if I fail, I am afraid that there will be divisions among us.'

With this Hoopoe declined the position. The other birds did not understand and they felt that everything was going wrong. There was no other way now to choose a leader than by the casting of lots. Each kind of bird cast a lot and sure enough the lot fell on Hoopoe's name. Now he had no excuse to give them, for his knowledge surpassed that of all the other birds. Unanimously they agreed that he was their leader and they covenanted to obey him. When Hoopoe accepted the role of leadership over the flock, all the birds were glad and said to him:

'You are our leader and as such, we will do whatever you want. You are our commander-in-chief, and we are your army. We will follow behind you anywhere you set out to go.'

LXVIII

The Birds are Bewildered when they Come to an Endless Valley, and One Bird Asks Hoopoe a Question

So after Hoopoe became their leader they preceded on their way, taking to the sky. They flew for several days and finally came to a place where they could stop. Before them they could see an endless valley. With this

sight, the birds' hopes were dashed, for this valley was as long as a lonely evening, separated from one's beloved, and it could be seen that it contained sorrows without end. Even to look upon it was like setting ones life and soul precariously on the brink of danger, however, there was no way but for the birds to cross it. Words cannot explain how tremendous and fearsome a sight it was. The birds were in torment and deeply afraid. At the sight of the mysterious valley, the birds' bodies became limp and their wings and tails drooped. Then one bird asked Hoopoe a question:

'Hey, why is this route barren?'

Hoopoe thought for a moment and answered:

'This route is free of the clamor of people as a sign that there is no need for a shah's honor and rank here.'

LXIX

A Story

One night Boyazid[44] emerged from his seclusion. It was a clear night and the moonlight shone all about. The blossoms of the stars formed a garden in the sky. The stars shone in the blue sky, bright like a perfect pearl in an azure sea. This Seventh Heaven resembled a splendid castle in the sky and with that the universe demonstrated its grandness. Surely, the mind is too feeble to truly comprehend the movement, peace, physique, and beauty of the heavens.

As this elder looked out from his vantage point, he was unable to spot even a trace of another living being. His desperate search for another person led him to the city, the mountains, and the wasteland. Nonetheless, he could not find a sign of anybody; he did not even encounter any helpless person apart from himself. Therefore, he said: 'O God! Why is this place void of people – people who feel pain and pleasure?'

Then he became aware of a secret that enthralled his mind: 'This is a place of honor and grandness, and not everyone is capable of finding their way here. This special place is intended for a shah; its sacredness has no bounds; were this land a person, no beggar could be a trustworthy servant

---

[44] See footnote 24 above.

for him. Those who dare to spend their lives on the road to this place will certainly face pain, but their arrival is never certain.

LXX

The Birds Ask Hoopoe Questions about the Valley of Difficulties and He Answers Them

After their guide spoke these words, the travelers grew anxious. They came across limitless problems and were subjected to burdensome suffering that seemed to have no end. They would see a road in front of them, a road that went on forever, with no end. The road had many problems and there was no solution to be found. Like a raging blaze, reaching to the sky, endangering heavens' very throne by its leaping flame, was the state of their grief. The wind of self-sufficiency danced so violently within the valley that the mighty sky's back was about to break.

How could feeble birds, afflicted in body and soul, make it past this terrible route? It is beyond comprehension! Their fear was so great that it blocked all sight of their soul. The birds that had succumbed to this difficult situation huddled around and in their immense weakness and desperation explained:

'O leader and greatest bird of all! God appointed you to be our guide. You should listen to our cries of weakness, since it is your duty. For you know this road well, and you are our guide in our waywardness. We are encountering too many difficulties on this road and we need you to realize this. We each desire to express our grievances and above all somehow be freed of them. We need you to elucidate our problems and tell us how to solve them. Your every word should be thorough and profound. They should chase away the doubts in our minds and clarify the upheaval in our soul. Purify all that is in our souls and vanquish the various hardships. Let not a speck of doubt remain in our hearts. The heart of the traveler should be still. Alight for a little while and bring calm to the perils that are threatening hearts of the flock. When each one speaks to you about their difficulty, give an answer that will bring resolution. There should remain no trace of fear in their hearts or worry in their minds, and then, when the road is made passable, we will set forth towards our goal with determination. Otherwise, the road won't pass quickly and it will be difficult for anyone to reach the end of it. In order to traverse

this road the heart should not be divided, for it is difficult to start this road already burdened with doubt.'

This idea seemed reasonable to the leader and so he said: 'Gather all birds that have questions in one place.' Thus he accepted the flock's request and found a broad spot to alight. All the other birds also alighted. Then under nothing more than the shelter of knowledge, they brought their questions before their mullah.

LXXI

One Bird's Question

As soon as Hoopoe said, 'Whoever has a problem should ask it now,' one of the birds with a question said:

'O dear bird of birds! You and we are of the same flock. All of our wings and feathers are equal. However, please tell us, why are you so aware of concealed secrets and we are not. Explain this from head to foot. Help us understand why this is so.'

LXXII

Hoopoe's Answer

Hoopoe's answer to those before him was:

'Solomon's eyes found me. With God's glance, Solomon became a prophet and king. God then, as a revelation of his mercy, appointed him shah of all the spirits, people, beasts, and birds. My humble and deprived state required the mercy of such a blessed king and for this reason I now have such a high crown. For whoever a pure-hearted person even glances at the very ground around that person will turn into gold.'

LXXIII

Shaikh Hajmiddin Kubro's Word and How
He Acknowledged a Dog

Shaikh Najmiddin Kubro was considered a great leader in his day.

If he noticed anybody taking pleasure in looking at him, his eyes would shine with rays of saintliness and then that person would fall unconscious and rising immediately with their own saintliness. The Shaikh's power was so great that even a mere glace of him could transform someone into a saint.

One day, when the Shaikh was drunk, a dog caught his eye. Once the dog tasted the savor of friendship with the Shaikh, he abandoned its dog-like behavior. It came up to the Shaikh and it put its head on his lap and announced his loyalty and in this way became a leader among dogs. Wherever the dog went in the city he was immediately surrounded by packs of dogs. Wherever he sat he reigned as the shah of dogs, and other dogs would place themselves around him like bodyguards.

When on the day appointed by destiny the dog died, a grave was dug not far from the Shaikh's door. They buried the dog there and marked the grave as if it were a person's tomb. In the shah-dog's wake the other mongrels formed a circle around his grave and howled at the top of their voices.

'Even today many believers lay their head on his grave and give alms. His grave is still preserved in the country of Khorezm[45] and the governor takes pleasure in this. Have you ever heard anything more interesting in the entire world? If a person notices a fortunate dog and the glance has a beneficial result, the dog will be given the characteristics of a person. Let this blessing not only give a dog semblance of humanity, but also the joy of the prophet's light!

'If the prophet was able to raise the status of a dog then it is clear that he is able to raise the status of a bird too. Is it strange if the prophet looks at a bird with mercy and then all other birds become subject to him? Stories like this have existed since ancient times and the story of 'Friends in the Cave'[46] is one example. If God is a giver of blessings, then it is no wonder that he can also provide for a dog or a bird!'

---

[45] A region in south-west Uzbekistan.

[46] According to this story, three important people escaped a cruel king and hid in the cave. They had a dog with them. The dog displayed loyalty to these people and since it was in the cave its name was also mentioned among those people.

LXXIV

Another Bird's Question for Hoopoe

With tears in his eyes, another bird came forward with this question:
'O emir of all the birds! The road is difficult and in my weakness I find that there is no one to help me. Surely, a fly cannot take the same course as Anqo. At every breath of this journey we met with hundreds of difficulties and causes of suffering appear all about us. This path must originate from the mountain of evil, for the whirlwinds that spring up from the road sling death's dust into our eyes. The howling winds sweep down from that mountain and snatch up stones as if they were soul. Even a lion treads this road with trepidation. So how is it possible for a puny ant to traverse it?'

LXXV

Hoopoe's Answer

Hoopoe said to him:
'O weak and impoverished one! Your spirit is low, and you are wasting away in your misery. It isn't right that your body should be so wounded and weak. This work is definitely a work of love. Therefore, since your spirit ought to be high why are you so sorrowful? Whoever is not in love is not human. The essential aspect of a person is love and many expectant people diligently seeking after it, but their efforts fall short. Destitute wanderers, who have no homes, show the outward signs of lovers in love since misery is the job of lovers. The thought constantly on their mind is the abandonment of their souls. They want to be free of worldly existence; thinking only of their soul mate rather than their life. For the one who is in love, what difference is it if his body is sick or well? Surely, to give his soul up in love is his purpose, for in love all problems are solved. If his purpose in love is death, he will see value in the disasters that have penetrated his soul. Whoever's heart is in this realm will be ill in mind and soul and the sickness of love will only do them harm. Those who are in love do not endorse this weakness, and yet, they consider it to be the source of their inspiration. Since the highest aspiration of love is to die, sickness is seen as something aiding in the pursuit of that end as it brings them closer to

death. However, sickness causes a person to abandon their spirit and how amazing it is for them to give such a thing up! No matter the reason, after they have met the requirement of abandoning their soul in love, they find it pleasant. If the result of sickness is the abandonment of one's soul than the sacrifice of the soul and the world are worthy of this death.

'If you live for one thousand years on the surface of this earth, one day you will succumb to death in sickness and sorrow. You cannot escape death. So, isn't it better to die as a direct result of love's desire? If your dream is to die on the road of devotion to your beloved, be assured that this is indeed eternal life!'

LXXVI

Shaikh Abu Said Abulkhair's[47] Story

The Shaikh from Mehna, Abu Said Abulkhair, was lucky enough to come across his beloved on the way. Initially, he felt a great need to be loved and thus the terror of the blade of a hundred evils loomed close by. These circumstances caused him to fall ill and as if someone were smothering the breath from his lungs his very existence seemed stifled. His sickness lingered and he gave way to weeping. Yet in this dark state, the flash of love's lightning set his soul ablaze and its flames of passion wrapped their fingers around his ravaged body. He could not sleep at night nor could he find peace during the day. He had nothing to claim as his own other than the illness of love's anxiety. During the day his mind and thoughts were on her and it became customary to wail and mourn the separation. At night he could not be contained in the city or gardens, but would wander towards the wasteland and the steep mountain peaks.

Far away, in a place hard to find, the Shaikh came across the ruins of a cabin that resembled an owl's fortress. The cabin had a very deep well and once a man of happiness drowned there. And now the Shaikh, overcome by the relentless waves of love, succumbing to his grief; shed blood from his eyes until dawn's arrival. He desired to die of love, but he could not find death's answer. On expectancy, however, he could not close his eyes in sleep and his resolution remained steadfast. The

---

[47] Abu Sayid Abdulkhair was a well-known Shaikh of Khorasan. He died in 1048.

torture made his body gaunt and his groans made his very soul raw. He remained in this distant place for years, and finally, his lips felt once for all the victory of union.

'Whoever considers himself to be a man when he falls in love should do likewise. For a man cannot obtain this wealth without relinquishing his life.'

LXXVII

Another Bird's Question for Hoopoe

One bird said:

'In my life I have committed many sins. My state of shamefulness is terrible. Defeated by the unclean work I once busied myself with, sorrow now crushes me, and these things impede my travel. Everybody knows that the things done by a mosquito that alights on rubbish are filthy. What kind of contact can I then have with the pure Semurgh? Purity is needed enter the presence of the Semurgh. One who is soiled by evil and lacks modesty cannot come near him. Someone may be pure, but my character is not and therefore, shame is keeping me from pursuing my desire to meet him.'

LXXVIII

Hoopoe's Answer

Hoopoe said to him:

'You have resigned yourself to the idea that you are covered in sin. You need to realize that you won't live in the world forever. In the end everyone who exists will die. If you want to die with your sin, people will want to laugh at you. You are very ignorant and before the wise people, illiterate.

'You use to dream of being free of your sins, well dreamer, this is something easy to achieve. The way to rid yourself of sin is simply to repent. Only repent and like a lamp in the darkness of rebellion's night there will be light.

'In this muck of sin there is no clean person to be found. Nobody has

ever known a sinless person. God did not create Adam's race sinless. O unaware person, whose sin will God pass over with clemency and grace if you don't repent? If anybody's face is paled by sin, repentance will still bring him life. For when the sea of grace washes over you, as it has me, you will be purified a hundred thousand times over.'

LXXIX

Pure Adam's Story

The righteous and eternal God created father Adam to be the predecessor of all the people in the world. God put the crown righteousness on his head and adorned it with the pearl of prophet-hood. His honor and rank were made so elevated that it is said that even the angels worshipped the ground beneath his feet. The apex of the sky was the ground under his feet and the garden of paradise was his place to shine. Therefore, he became worthy of great glory and esteem. God gave him the name of 'Safiy' which means 'pure'.

However, the powerful creator's sovereignty permitted Adam's face to become black with sin and rebellion. Adam lost his honor and worthiness and his deeds became unacceptable. Then an outstretched hand blocked his chest and he was exiled from the garden of paradise. His fate was a blackened face and he arrived in India homeless. He continued to weep in solitude for years, and everybody around heard his sighs and groans. Like the furious flame that consumes the parched grass of autumn, so his soul was ravaged by the guilt of the sins he had committed. Finally freedom from his torment came as he repented, and once again a gentle wind swept down from the garden of grace, breaking the bonds of a hundred thousand torments that once enslaved him. God accepted his penitence and he regained his former honor and position.

'If it was this easy for a sinful man such as this, who had horrendous torments, your situation can hardly compare. You are simply too weak to do what you need to in order to achieve your desire! Repent and attain your salvation through your penitence; complete the journey and attain your goal!'

LXXX

Another Bird's Question for Hoopoe

Another bird asked:

'O beauty of the crown! My character is marked by inconsistency. If anything can be said about me it is this. I am busy with sinful and immoral works and then I turn around and do righteous deeds. Sometimes I am crooked and sometimes I am truthful. Sometimes I am the companion of drinkers and sometimes I enjoy the company of those who lift their voices to God. Sometimes I am a worshipper of Allah and visit Ka'ba, and sometimes I worship in front of the idol in the idol-house. There is no stability in my life and so I greatly suffer. I need to realize that with my fluctuating, wicked character and these draining habits I cannot find the right way. For this journey is of one color. That is, if I am not wholly faithful, I will not be able to find myself.'

LXXXI
Hoopoe's Answer

Hoopoe replied:

'I tell you the truth everyone exhibits this repulsive attribute! It is caused by selfishness and conscience. As one of them is bound, the other will unfurl its bloom; if anyone denies their gluttony they will be overcome by spirituality. Every such person will possess glory, be considered pure, and lead a good life.

'In the case of one's nature being inclined to change, then like you he may meet shame. Through the lessons taught by difficulties and sickness he will learn resolution. If the dangers presented by voracity are too overwhelming, a person can also turn to the mullah's guidance. For a mullah is good at remedying all kinds of evils and that is why, O naïve one, people call him 'elder'. If a pupil of Sufism faces various trials due to his greed on this road of demand and consequently sins (it is undeniable that sometimes pupils face these kinds of problems), the mullah will treat him differently, thereby repelling evil and bringing healing. What you have expressed is surely this kind of sickness, the cure for which consists of abstinence. This labor should also be your aim. As if you were binding a

rope around a strong pillar, so cling to this source of might, since the hope of highest mercy will reveal itself here, releasing you from this lingering shame. Then you will rejoice in those difficulties and will walk on God's road as a pure traveler.'

LXXXII

Shaikh Abu Turab Nakhshabiy's[48] Story

Abu Turab Nakhshabiy set the standard for purity of nature and lived in union with God. Once he glanced upon a dervish and caught a glimpse of some jewelry on him. This dervish was wearing the clothes of a Sheikh, the material was new and his robes were decorated with green and yellow ornaments. His lust was for beauty and particularly the wearing of beautiful clothes.

In order to free him of his desire the elder prescribed many things for him to do, but his words were fruitless. When the elder realized that he could not overcome this attribute, he directed the dervish to be taken to the butcher's every day until his bad habits came to an end. He ordered sheep's intestines, still filled with feces, to be put into a basket, and the dervish's head to be held firmly in it until the torment was too much. And then he forced him to go through Nacaf[49] market, with his turban still dripping, so that all could see.

It took several days, but this measure did remedy his ornery lust. After this, not a trace of majesty remained on the 'Sheikh's' clothes and all his beauty was brought to naught. After the trials killed his lust the elder instructed the high pupil to wash properly. In this way he made him get rid of this sickness and pass through the peril safe and sound. Now, since he made his place the hall of union whatever he wished came true.

'Make your lusts go through trials and when you look again, instead of your lusts you will find treasure. Otherwise you are as good as dead in the hell of transience.'

---

[48] A prominent Shaikh of Qarshi, which is now a major city in southern Uzbekistan

[49] 'Nacaf' is the ancient name of the modern city Qarshi. With using this word Navoiy was also hinting at the word 'Nafac' which in Chag'tai means the driving force of people, their lust.

LXXXIII

Another Bird's Question for Hoopoe

A bird queried:

'O blessed one! Lust is cruel to me and like an opponent, stands in my way. Whatever is ordered, the opposite is done and none of these evil deeds can be forgiven. What will I do if my lust is my enemy on this path? How can I travel this difficult way?'

LXXXIV

Hoopoe's Answer

Hoopoe said:

'O weakling who is given to self-indulgence! The tyranny of lust has wounded your soul. Although you condemn your lust day and night, it is clearly senseless chatter meant to be a balm to your guilty soul. I say this because you do whatever lust orders. It has overcome you and won complete victory. In fact, you do nothing without its order. Whatever fancy it has, you are ready on your feet to carry it out. Your life is spent carrying out its wishes. Wherever it dreams to go, you follow right behind. Just like the harness on a mule, lust rides on your back, turning your head as it wills. Wherever it leads, you follow; when it says, 'Go' you go and when it says 'Stop' you stop.

In the limitless play and laughter of your childhood you became lust's captive. You sank into ignorance and the years of your youth with it, you didn't realize even for a moment what was best for yourself. Now you have come to old age and you cannot throw off your old habits; you are still busy engaging in debauchery and rebellion. You have spent your entire life in this state of ignorance and defiance. Now, possessing one hundred thousand desires, the time of death has come. Although you have lived through many days, you have never thought of God's orders at all, and you have nothing to claim as your own besides the path of waywardness and sin. If one searches the world over, it is not possible to find a person like you who has spent their life in such vanity. When you were alive you were deep in ignorance, but when you die you will see your state clearly.'

LXXXV

A Story

There once lived a cruel shah who was a drunkard and found no shame is his tyranny or love of killing. His dirty lust would command him to do various evil exploits and he always obeyed, even going above and beyond what was asked. One day, when he was in his usual state of inebriation, he saw two dervishes clothed in robes pass him on the street. It was apparent that they were friends, the closest of confidants, as they showed concern and sympathy towards each other. The shah called one of them aside and asked the following question of one of them about his companion:

'Tell me, what is your relationship with your friend comprised of?'

The Dervish answered the shah:

'The nature of our friendship consists of our being friends, helpful to one another, being likeminded, and supporting each other.'

Being ignorant and drunk the shah challenged:

'O owner of the way, tell me, do you like me or do you like your friend?'

The Dervish answered:

'First, I will tell you what I know about the two of you. After you find out about it, O owner of a crown, you can judge for yourself. Although you reign as shah over many people, you have strayed from God's road. Whatever God orders you to do, you do the opposite, and you are constantly passing your life in a state of ignorance. As for my companion, although he is a dervish and beggar, he fulfills God's orders completely. He has not once left the right road. He spends his time accomplishing God's orders. You are a king, but your lust has left you desolate and a slave, while that beggar has enslaved his lust. It will continue like this until you each meet your death since it is your way of life. After death, my friend will become a shah and you will become a beggar, for while you were being drunk he was a traveler of the right road.'

LXXXVI

Another Bird's Question for Hoopoe

Another bird asked:

'The damned devil decided to ensnare me using his cunning and craftiness. He does not let me rest for a moment and fetches various worlds of things for my heart to ruminate. With every moment he shoves thought after thought into my mind, and it is impossible to get rid of him. Since I cannot be free of him I have to do what he dictates. My condition is so helpless because his constant temptations leave my mind too weak to cast them aside.'

LXXXVII

Hoopoe's Answer

Hoopoe said:

'To the extent that your lust is alive, the devil will hide in it and be its assistant. Lust has put so much pride in your heart that it chokes your soul. Even Satan will be astonished when he sees it and will wander, stumbling in his shock, through the Valley of Disbelief. Satan uses whatever areas in your life that lust has overcome. He smirks whenever you do something by the order of your lust. Do not tell Satan that you are desperate because then he will even use your lust as his ambassador. All works and events related to the world are related to Satan. God created your lust such that it is exposed to one hundred of Satan's crafts. However, your lust shows such trickery and deceit that it would put even a hundred devils to shame. Why are you complaining of Satan while this kind of lust accompanies you?'

LXXXVIII

A Story

A disciple who had lost hope that his prayers would be answered entered the presence of Shaikh Kharaqoni[50] and said:

'Satan deceives me in many ways as a hindrance to my love and labor.

---

[50] Abulhasan Kharaqoni was a Shaikh of Khurson. He died 1033-34.

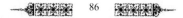

Therefore, my prayers are impeded and all the prayers that I have made are useless.'

The wise mullah gave him this reply:

'O taskmaster, you slash Satan's soul with the blade of your oppression. He also complained of your domination and told me all about your oppression and tyranny. He said: "I was initially destined by God to make people's condition desolate through deceit. I lead people to rebellion and to the Valley of Shortcomings. Then you commissioned a dervish with such bad qualities that they even exceeded mine. Every time the beggars came near him, I contemplated placing temptations in his heart, but then saw that his heart was already occupied with every evil that I could have enticed him with. Moreover, even filthy deeds that I had not thought of were already at home in his mind.'

'Satan said these things about you and gave us a copious amount of praise. On account of your cunningness and craftiness we thank you greatly, for Satan himself thanked your learned elder.

The dervish replied:

'Satan has slandered me, and he was the one who led me to evil works.'

The Shaikh retorted:

'You are doing good work, not excluding you're contention with Satan. I was the one who listened to your excuses and was your judge. Shame on you a hundred times on behalf of Satan!'

LXXXIX

Another Bird's Question for Hoopoe

The bird asked:

'O owner of blessed beauty! The wealth of limitless love was invested in my heart. The idea of utilizing it makes my soul rejoice and when like coins in the purse of my heart I hear it jingling my heart finds peace. The moment that there is no gold or silver in my heart's purse, you may as well declare me dead.'

Hoopoe's Answer

Hoopoe said to him:

'O one who is far from truth! Money is the cause of your grief as you are far gone from it. Greed's goblet makes your heart drunk, and from this drunkenness you will became one with the ground. Who says these kinds of things? This is not the work of honest people – true people are ashamed of it. This dirty work is only right for rodents. It always tries its best to dig but has to live in poverty with the dirt. On account of its malicious greed, it digs various holes underground and suffers greatly from its evil habits. In this way it digs and finds a hole leading to a house. But then suddenly a hidden cat pounces on it from the shadows of the corner, savoring the rodent's meat as he gnaws and swallows its blood. Or your likeness can be found in a snake lying on top of a treasure for years on end. In exchange for the wealth people will give it an appropriate punishment, that is, when people see its eyes they will immediately stomp on its head. Hey dirt, you are also like that. You remind your generation of either a snake or a rodent. You know what the consequences are and you should know that this quality of yours is far from good.

'The one who likes silver and gold will be its slave and drunk from its enticement. Picture a cruel, ignorant, drunk person who upon seeing silver or gold bows in worship before it, his idol. Of this kind of person it can be said that he has abandoned Islam in ignorance and gone to Hell. In this world's garden he will endure difficulties as long as he lives. He will pine after gold and silver and in the end die in misery.

'Very well, let me not call you a rodent; let me consider you to be equal to Qorun.[51] And let me not call you a snake; let me call you Faridun.[52] However, how will it end? What have they done and what can you do? Regardless, you will have to leave your wealth in this world and join the majority. Therefore, expel the useless thoughts from your head. Save your mind from the labor of carrying this hard stone of great weight. If you are a true person, focus on the original goal and say what you should say. Do not occupy yourself with inappropriate work because it will harm

---

[51] See footnote 17 above.
[52] See footnote 16 above.

you and ultimately kill you.'

XCI

A Story

There lived a miser in Basra.[53] He was ignorant and occupied himself by collecting gold and silver. If Hotam Tai[54] is famous for his generosity, this man was even more famous for hoarding coins. That cruel and petty person suffered much, yet one by one obtained his precious silver pieces. Once he had saved a considerable treasure, he buried it. This harsh man also had his robe stuffed with a comparable amount of treasure. In the eyes of that greedy man, his copious treasure, although hidden, glittered like stars in the sky even in the bright light of day. He even reasoned to himself that the strength in his body and the health that marked his life were on account of his wealth.

One day he came to do business at the seaside. Having traded his goods, with his dirty money, he bought something to eat. After that he wanted to wash his hands and so he knelt by the river's bank. The riches sewn into his clothes were cumbersome and as he knelt, they suddenly pulled him into the water. That miser began to sink and all because of his covetousness. He was crying and flaying about in the water, shouting out in hope that somebody would come to help him. However, before people could come and help he had already sunk. As his anchor comprised of riches was so heavy he dropped to the very bottom of the water, like a pearl in its shell resting on the ocean floor.

'The very wealth that he had hoarded was the very thing that brought about his demise. In addition, his hidden treasure was pillaged. The procurement of gold and silver ends in a dreadful manner. Pull you hands away from such revolting work! Never show your desire to them because this labor is a sea of nothingness, and the world's terrifying waves are capable of destroying it.'

---

[53] A port city in southern Iraq.

[54] Hotam Tai lived in the second half of the sixth century and belonged to the Arab Tai tribe. He was famous for his generosity and in Eastern literature is a symbol of generosity.

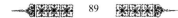

XCII

Another Bird's Question for Hoopoe

The bird asked:

'O owner of high rank! I live in a place like Paradise; every tree therein looks as tall and stately as a tree of Paradise. On all sides clear springs flow like the river of Paradise. The water of that place is sweet, its air pleasant, and the fruit of the trees give energy and health to everyone who eats them. The area is as wide as the garden of Paradise and a huge castle was built in the middle of it. The castle was decorated with beautiful patterns inlaid with jewels and within it a handsome king resides. My abode is in that wonderful flower garden and here I have found union with the shah. He does not have conversations without me. Night and day I am his closest companion and confidant. Is it worth it to give up happiness such as this and start to seek Semurgh?'

XCIII

Hoopoe's Answer

Hoopoe said to him:

'O owner of empty ideas! What you said has no worth. Although the garden is beautiful, its water and air are pleasant to your eyes, the trees tower overhead like the trees of Paradise, and the flowers hold captive one's gaze with their one hundred coquetries, you should know that the open white lilac and the other flowers will disappoint you. Cypresses and hyacinth are not eternal here. In one day its spring, in a violent transition, passes into autumn, and the tender petals of the flowers fall and in their decay mingle with the black ground. The fortune's volatility will eventually bring destruction to the castle, and then your heart will be like that of a tortured lover. And the problems of the house will be so enormous that they will bring down the shah of the throne. Like beauties loyalty there is no loyalty in his garden; the shah's compassion like stone beauties is not forever.

'Who then are you in comparison with beauties, O weakling? You do not endure the poke of any flower's thorn in the garden! If you have real courage, prove it by going to the eternal mountain of Qof and join the shah who lives on the peak of that mountain. He has made a perfect garden

there. The reason why a garden's leaves fall and vanish is connected to him. The shah is charmed by his garden's beauty and counts it among his most prized possessions. A shah's loss of throne and greatness is also because of it. A shah's castle prospers because of his oversight, but then it is destroyed due to his power.'

XCIV

A Story

There lived a wandering dervish who was famous for his indolence. He smoked hashish from morning till late. He resembled a dervish who had shaken the world off from his coat tails; however, his secrets were hidden in the hashish container at his side. When he smoked hashish he did not know where to put himself, but this was his dream, to lead a carefree life.

One day he made his way into a ruin and there smoked hashish – more than his normal amount. Leaning against a broken wall he embarked on a trip into the world of secrets. He imagined that he was happy in a wonderful garden. He saw pleasurable things on all sides and this place of serenity appeared to be a magnificent palace. The building of the castle was decorated in the manner of the studio of the renowned painter Moni.[55] He saw himself seated upon a throne and a girl with beauty that radiated from her face like the rays of the sun, sat by his side. His majesty was busy enjoying life and every moment the beautiful girl was a delight to him. With these apparitions he was convinced that he was in the castle, yet all the time he was still lying in the ruin.

However, there was a scorpion with a slender stinger, its deadly venom ready at the tip. It came out to walk around the ruin and with each step, its stinger swayed to and fro. Then, while the slothful man, in his subconscious thought he was kissing the beautiful girl in the castle, the scorpion jabbed its spear! The dervish stood up on his feet screaming, and around him he saw only strife and vexation, not a garden, nor a palace with a throne, nor a beautiful girl. In this way his vain thoughts had found an end, but he had the fatal stinger his lip. He understood that what he had done was wrong, but his regret did not do him any good.

---

[55] A legendary talented painter and architect from the East.

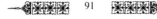

'You are also in a situation similar to his, as useless thoughts shroud your mind. One day you will be startled by a fatal sting and awaken from the sleep of ignorance. At that time your remorse will be of no use. Then will you understand whom you are far from, but by that time your soul will have no choice but to bear the scar of separation forever.'

XCV

Another Bird's Question for Hoopoe

A bird asked:

'O one without equal! Love has captured my soul. If I don't see my beauty's face, even for a single instant, the whole world immediately becomes dark in front of me. I cannot have peace if I am without her for one moment; therefore, I do nothing but suffer from sadness. My one aim in life is to look at her face, for when I meet her, my heart finds rest. I am such a companion of hers that to be separated from her causes me pain. If I don't hear her pleasant voice the bird of my spirit will bid farewell to my body. My soul is sick because of separation and my life is tied to meeting her. If I am deprived of her, my soul faces vexation and my heart laments day and night. I cannot be apart from her for a moment. If I am away from her it will be my death. Why should I leave the love of that beauty? Where should I go when I am separated from her?'

XCVI

Hoopoe's Answer

Hoopoe said:

'O one whose task is to burn with desire! Your heart flames with a lesser love. You are far from true love. The blemish of separation covers your heart. Your heart is astray in its love and yet thinks it has taken a good path. You try to quench your thirst by drinking from a dirty puddle, oblivious to the well of life that you could quench your thirst with. Your soul was unaware of the shiny pearl and was attracted by simple dewdrops. Turning your face from the shining sun in the sky, you were content with a candle and its rays. Chasing after illusive forms you deprive yourself of content's beauty. If you find beauty in a face of mucus and blood, what

will the result of your external beauty be later? Why do you praise the beauty of Chigil[56] girls? Don't you know that the blush and pall of their faces is merely blood and mucus?

'External beauty is not faithful; it changes and is not eternal. That's why it is not worth being in love for this since you will be spoiled by it. If anybody does not have lasting beauty, the beauty that she does have will be begged away by somebody else and be used only momentarily. Beauty that is beautiful one day and ugly the next is not be pleasant. Instead, you should love the owner of perfect beauty whose sun is never blighted. Even if she has one hundred thousand lovers like you, their love is not worthy of her. If each lover would sacrifice their soul one hundred times it would not be enough, because her beauty is worth one hundred thousand more.'

XCVII

A Story

Aristotle had a pupil that attended every lesson of his master's. The wise philosopher paid special attention to him and esteemed him more than his other pupils. He brought him up from childhood and taught him the secret knowledge that he possessed. He was the wisest pupil among the scholar's four hundred students and was only lesser than Aristotle. The scholar dreamed of making him Alexander the Great's future adviser. 'If I leave for anywhere, he can take my place at Alexander's court as my son,' he thought. This pupil was so wise that he could even debate with Plato.

One day, as he was passing by a street, a girl's love found the way to his heart. The girl, who was from the infidel's church, had a face as attractive as the moon and a body like silver, yet she was cruel like a stone-hearted infidel. Her allurement could massacre the peoples of one hundred religions and torment the wise, so great was her beauty!

When she caught the philosophy pupil, he fell deeply in love with her. He resolved to meet her and employed the aid of middlemen to arrange their rendezvous. Finally, after great expense, he was able to favorably incline himself to her and marry her. After he accepted union with this

---

[56] One of the names of an old Turkic tribe. Chigil girls were famous for their beauty.

idol he became an idolater like the infidels, that is, he could not go far away from her. Night and day he did not take his eyes off her, and being charmed, completely fascinated with her, he stopped reading books. He was so ravished by her beauty that he even forgot to attend his master's classes. Realizing what was happening to him, his master searched for a way to help him. He presented the pupil with a great deal of advice, but it did not help. The master saw that his pupil's knowledge and wisdom, which he had accumulated for years was wasting away. It is not known how long this matchless philosopher was lost in contemplation, but he still could not find a cure for his pupil's malady. At last he thought of a covert measure and gave the beauty a strong drug without her knowing. When the beauty swallowed it she cried out and sank to the ground. As time passed her state worsened.

The boy tried different means of treatment for her, but nothing helped – the idol would not recover. After suffering this misfortune of failing to find the way to health for his beloved, the young student came before his master in great sorrow. Hanging his head with shame he explained the situation to his master. When he saw his pupil's plight, he went to the sick girl for the purpose of curing her. He said to his pupil:

'Get up and do your service to your master today; show your gratitude to Alexander. I will take care of your patient and heal your beautiful companion.'

Accepting his master's words, the pupil set off and the master began treating the invalid. He prepared a strong medicine to cleanse the stomach and she swallowed it. The master ordered his attendants to carefully watch her and hold a basin ready under the door of her mouth. They were not to pour out whatever she vomited, but rather protect her basin.

After he said this and had departed, the drug took effect. The medicine squeezed out the sputum that had brought on the girl's illness. She began vomiting without ceasing. During this whole time the master was out. The invalid had neither strength nor a drop of blood remain in her body. When she got rid of the sputum, bile, bad blood, and love she became very weak like a pale beauty.

In the evening the young man returned home, whereupon the wise man said to him, 'Enter and see your soul-mate!' The pupil entered the house to see his sinful and yet pleasant soul mate. The vision that met his eyes however, was that of a shrunken unconscious body in the place where his

beloved should be resting. Not recognizing her he asked, 'Where is my sweetheart? Where is my tulip with the figure of a cypress?' When the wise man heard this, knowing the depths of everything he heard, he replied, 'Bring the basin and give it to the beauty's lover.' The ones who heard his order brought the basin. It was full of various vomit and other foul smelling bodily excretions. The master looked at his pupil and said:

'Here, take this – it is your fairy! This is your flower face beloved. What you were afflicted with was nothing more than this. This is what you loved and were fascinated with.' With these words from his master, the pupil was mortified before him.

Seeing his pupil in this uncomfortable situation the master tried to reassure him:

'O my child, it was out of necessity that I found this way to treat you – not her. You are one who fell in love, and she is your sweetheart, the soul mate that charmed you. However, this kind of love, O depressed one, is shameful in the eyes of people who posses pure love!'

XCVIII

Another Bird's Question for Hoopoe

With woe another bird asked:

'O knower of hidden secrets! I am afraid of perishing on this road. I could loose my life before I reach the destination. How can I bear this enormous peril that opposes?'

XCIX

Hoopoe's Answer

Hoopoe said to him:

'O weakling whose soul is blind! Think it over; you cannot stay forever in this world. Whoever comes into this world will leave shaking off their coat tails, and death's blade will pierce their chest. Scholars have proven that this seemingly endless life ultimately finishes with death. Only illiterate and mindless people are oblivious to the fact that this event that

will occur. It does not matter whether you live one thousand years or only one instant, death will never bring you safety. Even a saint cannot escape its vortex, likewise a prophet cannot be free of its centripetal force. Regardless of how much a person is afraid or grieved they cannot be free of its force. There is no way to elude it or bribe it to give you release from its claim. Death's blade will accomplish its severity. It does not matter if you cry or beg there is no way to depart from this road. This road ends for both the hermit and the scoundrel, for the shah and the beggar. There is no use in fearing it! Indeed, there are already more than enough causes for anxiety. Since there is no way to avoid death, one should listen and pay it heed.'

C

A Story

They say that once the top star of the high envoy of Solomon reclined atop Solomon's throne during one of the days that he resided as prophet over the land. Giants and fairies alike were waiting for his command, as were all the other beings of the world; people, wild animals, and birds were ready in his service. All of them happy to fulfill his orders and hopeful to carry out his good works.

A wise man was dejectedly standing in silence before him. At that moment, an angel flew down to the prophet. It was Azrael, the executioner of heaven. After he bowed and gave his greetings to the prophet, the angel of death made this complaint:

'O pride of merciful people! The wisdom of God is so mysterious that even intelligence is astonished by it. Look, this dear person who is standing before you has been sentenced to death. He is about to die as a sentence has come from on high. At this hour I must stab his side with the dagger of execution, slaying him in India - how extremely surprising and terrifying!'

While Azrael was saying these words, the aforementioned man knelt before the prophet, kissed the ground, and with weeping said:

'O great prophet! I am greatly surprised by my circumstances today and my thoughts are incoherent due to death's terror. Find a way for me to leave this country, because my eyes are growing dim from terror.'

At that Solomon ordered the wind: 'Take him to the place that he wishes! Place him wherever he desires to stop and dispel the anxious feelings of

his heart.' The wind swiftly swept up his whole body and he directed the wind towards India. When they got there he did not go further. He said: 'Let me have a rest here because I like this place.' Having said this, the rider descended, but his swift horse continued on the wind's route. When Azrael arrived at his destination, he gave praise to God's omnipotence and ushered the rider into the presence of the other deceased. Azrael's job is to take souls, even those who flee with the wind.

<h1 style="text-align:center">CI</h1>

Another Bird's Question for Hoopoe

The bird asked:

'O one of unadulterated lineage! I tried hard all my life, but I could not achieve my goal and instead I've experienced sorrow and grief. A traveler upon this road should be light-hearted, able to laugh; someone who is not hardened by the world's hardships. As for me, life's worries make me distressed. My soul is always hurting due to some grief. By what happiness of mine can I traverse this road? How can I go to the place where glad-hearted people go?'

<h1 style="text-align:center">CII</h1>

Hoopoe's Answer

Hoopoe said to him:

'O sorrowful one! It is your destiny to have grief as your excuse, while real people accept grief as the food for the journey through this valley. To suffer from this road's sorrows is the fitting labor of courageous people. A person who does not suffer on the road is not a true person. The courageous rejoice in suffering. This kind of captivity is their freedom. When they get to the bottom of suffering they find this world, whose passage is nothing other than sorrow. Here every person is doomed to some kind of grief. Those who are close to the people of the world are always ready to suffer the road's sorrows for their sake. If it is not possible to alleviate the whole world's sorrow, then it is always good for humanity to alleviate individual sorrow. If you have suffered, O sorrowful one, enter this road and make yourself happy. If you are grieved by the latter,

be happy because your heart will prosper from it. People who know love can rejoice even in suffering. How strange it is that their very desire is for that which is undesirable! To reach the goal you need to endure the road of suffering; only these difficulties can liberate your heart. Whoever does not have these difficulties is not real. For only by the sustenance of suffering is this road traversable.'

CIII

A Story

There was a highly generous person in Egypt who was the owner of the realm of meaning. He had everything needed for carousing. He had a hundred times more than what you would think would be needed. He lived in a palace like Paradise and the sweetheart that accompanied him had the beauty of the women of Paradise. However, this man with high purity did not care about these things. Like Joseph trapped in the dungeon of separation, grief and sorrow accompanied him all the time.

He was asked:

'O pure one whose soul is full of sorrow. Inform us of your dark secret. Why aren't you happy? You have everything for merrymaking. Why does your soul feel nothing but sorrow?

The man answered:

'For those of the road this world is a dungeon, because their dream is hidden from their eye. The main work for a person is to cover all the roads and reach their soul's desire. Is it possible for a person to be happy in a dungeon? How can a person be free of sorrow while in the house of sorrow?

I suffer from the unfulfilled desire of my real beloved, God. Therefore, even though I am in the Garden of Eden, I consider myself to be in a dungeon. I won't be able to be free of the concerns of sorrow until I reach his flower garden of union.'

CIV

Another Bird's Question for Hoopoe

The bird asked:

'O incomparable one! I live to fulfill of God's commands; I am always

ready for his orders and it is all the same to me whether he is furious with it or shows his blessing. Whatever he orders I will carry out, and he alone decides whether to reject it or accept it. Whatever he orders, whether it is summer or winter, I will do it. It is not my business whether he rejects it or accepts it. My duty is to do what he orders and if I fulfill it I'm happy.'

CV

Hoopoe's Answer

Hoopoe said to him:

'What you have expressed is praiseworthy and although what you have said may be true, it would be better if others said this for you rather than you saying it. For the ever-living God destined people to achieve perfection on this road. Whoever obeys his orders and fulfills it, his rank will be exalted on this road. Conversely, whoever goes against his commands and rejects them will be sent away from God's high castle. The fulfiller of his orders will have a blessed future and will be known as a righteous person; his aim will be to obey God's commands and will not have any peace without it.

'If anybody obeys or prays according to the decrees, and yet boasts of his own work and is arrogant, for this reason his soul will meet disaster. Whether he prays early or late, a little or a lot, all his prayers will be as nothing. Whoever does not consider what he has done and is not arrogant, even counting his prayers as nothing, this person will enter the street of happiness, and his acts of righteousness and supplications will find use. Such a person will taste of their prayers and virtue and be satisfied by the meaning of their work.'

CVI

A Story

Before God created Adam and put the candle's spirit into his body, all the angels prayed, lived uprightly, and submitted to God's prescribed forms and rituals. Satan, as their guide, led the hosts of angels in all these rites and helped them find ease when they faced difficulties. He obeyed God's orders and busied himself in prayer to God for several thousand years.

One cannot adequately describe his deeds in this sphere and it is difficult to even imagine the extent of them! They say that there was no place in the whole world or the nine heavens of space where Satan had not placed his face to the ground in prayer.

Then, God created Adam and made him the one dear to his heart – he grew to love him greatly. He ordered all the angels to praise Adam, who was the best of all people. After such a command was given to the angels, they praised holy humanity. Satan, however, constrained by the vanity in all that he had done for thousands of years on end - his righteous works and prayers completed in perfect acquiescence to God's command – disregarded Adam and refused to praise him. Therefore, God likewise rejected him, expelling him from the host of angels. He deprived him of the pleasure he once found in praying and placed a cursed stone around his neck. His several thousand years of praying proved to be in vain and he was exiled from the place of God.

'You should understand this well that God considers there to be no other sin than self-centeredness and arrogance. To see oneself is to see prayer, and to mention what one has done is to be arrogant.'

CVII

Another Bird's Question for Hoopoe

The bird said:

'O exalted one! What will a pure lover on God's road find as a reward? This is hidden to me; please explain it. For on this road I have achieved purity. I have humbly worshipped and so have reached this.'

CVIII

Hoopoe's Answer

Hoopoe replied:

'This work is difficult, but it will be easy for one who is God's beloved. If each person of elevated character obtains this wealth, there will be no more need for food on this road. That is, the nourishment of this road is non-nourishing. It is necessary for a person to be free of any subjection to food; one who chooses this road is required to put godliness, profit, and

loss completely aside and let it be purified in the fire of nothingness of God's way, and with joy he should let them burn and turn into ashes. All this ash should rise up into the air and not a trace remain.

'With the help of a volatile spring wind, he may then completely cast out of his heart all that he has done. Whatever he has done before, he must rid himself of its claim upon him. If he is able to set his body aside in this way, then he can start upon this road.

'They say that if he is highly cognizant this road will consist of only one stride for him. This step requires the complete obliteration of everything through fire, so that not even a trace of what was there or was not there remains. Once he steps on this road, he will reach his desire and separation will disappear and he will copulate with his lover.'

CIX

A Story

There was a man whose name was Shah Ibrahim ibn Adham.[57] His journey's task was to surrender everything. He was a mullah on God's way and a pure person who was a devoted lover. On this road he relinquished his wealth, throne, country and the crown that once rested on his head, and with one thousand pleas he clothed himself in the rags of a dervish.

The honest lover and drunkard started traveling. He went from Balkh to Nishapoor, bringing ruin to the place he left and beauty to the place he entered. This pearl chose that mine of a place, making its mountain his home for seven years.

Here in his new home, he fasted during the day and prayed from dawn till dusk. In the daytime he also gathered an armful of firewood and twigs, which he took and sold at the market. With his earnings, he bought food for a meal to break his fast at dusk. As a result of his self-imposed difficulties, his body became emaciated.

One day while he was carrying a heavy load of firewood to the market to sell, a group of mullahs blocked his way to discover what benefit he found from being alone. One of them struck him with his fist. The one who had entered the way of poverty and nothingness said to them:

'What you seek is in Balkh, for although I came here, it remained there.'

---

[57] A well-known Shaikh who gave up shahdom for Sufism. He died in 777.

The examiners said: 'He has not reached it yet, it is still not dry under the wood as evidenced by the fact that he still has not forgotten Balkh. He needs to endure difficulties for several more years, maybe then he will forget about his possessions.'

After a year, the same small group of people wanted to examine him and so they met him on the road. According to the requirements of the examination one of them struck him with their fist. But this time the traveled sultan did not make a sound. Seeing this, the examiners cried: 'He has now reached his goal and has became perfect in his sect.' They expressed their praise and introduced themselves to the sultan. Later the mullahs and the shah accompanied each other on a trip to visit Ka'ba. Then the shah lost his shahdom and the travelers were well aware of this. If he had anything else in his memory, like a curtain, it would have obstructed his view of divine secrets. When everything in his memory disappeared, there was no longer a curtain, and he was able to return to his old house and former honor.

'For whoever reaches this kind of nothingness, O owner of easy envy, you should know, they alone can be called a true lover of God!'

CX

Another Bird's Question for Hoopoe

Another bird asked:
'O watchful one! I am a master of great generosity. If it is advantageous for people to be generous, then surely I should know something of its benefit. I am weak, but my generosity is great. What can be said about the one who understands the gist of meanings?'

CXI

Hoopoe's Answer

Hoopoe gave him the following answer:
'If this claim of yours is true, you will find great benefit from it on this road. If poor people are very generous their honor and position will be in accordance with it. If generosity is a pearl, then consider humanity to be

the beautiful mother-of-pearl and this mother-of-pearl to be honored by the pearl of charity. When a person is generous, throne and position are not needed; moreover, wealth and possession seem unpleasant. If anybody does not have wealth, it is enough for him to have generosity, as that constitutes his great assets. A generous person can accomplish anything.

Generosity makes any true person noteworthy, regardless of rank, possession, or treasure. Conversely, if a man has wealth and is not generous, those who have understanding will not think highly of him. Whoever is a master of openhandedness, that quality will bring him fortune. If a shah is poor in generosity then it is better to have a highly generous beggar than such a shah. You see, if a shah is lower in terms of generosity than a beggar, the vagabond will defeat him.

People's beauty is in their generosity and likewise they will receive punishment from their veracity.

Even if a person low in generosity finds what he thinks is high happiness, like a person low on the mountain of joy it has no value. A hired shepherd earns money for guarding and feeding one thousand sheep, yet if there is a wolf to endanger the herd than in this case it is better to have a dog than a shepherd who only works for money. For the person who has wealth but not generosity, this proverb about the shepherd and sheep can serve as an example. There is no difference between a man who guards treasure and that shepherd. Eventually, a generous drunkard will get the wealth and give it away to a beggar. If the drunkard is really a master of generosity and mercy it is just as easy for him to give away the whole treasure just as it is to spend it.

CXII

A Story

Writers have written the following about generous people:

On Judgment day everybody rose from their tombs. Both eremites and evildoers, both beggars and the affluent, all stood before the Judge on that day.

The highly honored elder Jom Shaikhi,[58] like a drunken live elephant

---

[58] Ahmadi Jom was a great Persian-Tajik poet. He died in 1141. Ahmadi Jomi's nickname was 'Live Elephant' ('Zinda Pil').

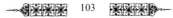

stepped out and with the eye of exhortation, stared one by one at the people who lay in Hell. He saw that various people were given different punishments, and he couldn't help but thinking about the sea of his generosity. He begged God to release the people from their torture, saying:

'O God! Forgive the sins of the people who are in Hell – the old and the young, the rich and the poor, the upper class and the lower class. Forgive; show mercy and release them from Hell! It is easy for you to do and it makes no difference to you whether they exist or not. If you do not accept my suggestion, then make my body such that I could fill all of Hell with it, for if your aim is to torture them then let me take the place of those who are weaker than I!'

This master of magnanimity, a generous drunkard, appealed to God like this on the Day of Judgment. Therefore, whoever is practiced in this kind of liberality, a worthy prize similar to this will be presented in exchange for it. When the legendary bird of generosity spreads his wings, one hundred thousand people find salvation in the protection of their shadow.

CXIII

Another Bird's Question for Hoopoe

A bird asked:

'O pure traveler, if a person has conscientiousness, what good comes from it? I was condemned to be honest and this provision alone feeds my soul. If a person has this quality will he be able to reach God?'

CXIV

Hoopoe's Answer

Hoopoe said:

'Ah, this is good talking. People value this habit. There are many praiseworthy qualities people may possess, but the most glorious one of them all is conscientiousness. Whoever does not speak honestly is not considered a real person. Dishonesty is the worst defect that can mar a one's nature.

'This quality is the work of the truly brave, and not everyone can take hold

of it. A person does not need to seek honesty instead he is to be concerned with giving it. Those of truth do not need sincerity from others, because they posses sincerity in themselves. In other words, if one is not truthful, they will demand that others speak the truth, thus in their distrust they reveal that they are actually dishonest people.'

CXV

A Story

A man with the nickname of Porso,[59] was famous for his high position and religious deeds. He went on a journey to visit Mecca setting out in the direction of the Islamic holy place, Ka'ba. Hoja Abu Nasr[60] was this Hoja's[61] servant, son and closest friend. When they reached their destination, they gave thanks to God. Whatever duties there were, they fulfilled it, and their goal was to aid other people's pilgrimage, by making it acceptable with their prayers. People in support of their purpose sought out Hoja in order to make their work acceptable. Some six hundred thousand searchers and travelers for God made this request of Hoja.

Like the author of 'Purity' and 'Knowledge'[62] Hoja looked at the community and gave this answer:

'Since you asked me to do this work, I will not abjure my promise. However, the one who carries out this work should be uniquely gifted with holiness and honesty and therefore this duty is not mine. Rather look to Abu Nasr, for he is your connection. He is pure. Let him pray for those who are captured.'

And so, with this introduction Hoja Abu Nasr recommended to pray for the people. The people embraced his honesty and goodness and Hoja Abu Nasr ascended the rostrum to pray over the people. In order to fulfill the task the people had set before him, he begged before God on their account. And Hoja could be heard continually saying, in all sincerity,

---

[59] Porso was a famous Bukhara Shaikh. Hoja Muhammad Porso was also known as Bahovuddin Naqshbandi. He died in 1419.

[60] Hoja Abu Nasr was Hoja Muhammad Porso's son. He died in 1460..

[61] 'Hoja' is a honorific title that distinguishes a person as a descendent of Muhammad's lineage. This title is still used in Central Asia. In this story 'Hoja' in the singular refers to 'Porso', the father

[62] In Uzbek they are titled 'Qudsiya' and 'Faslul-Khitab.'

'amen' beside the rostrum. When the prayer finally came to an end, the one who was on the rostrum said:

'O powerful God! Even if my prayers are not acceptable, then at least you should not waste the 'amens' of the one standing below!'

Hearing this, six hundred thousand people began wailing, big and small alike. People praised them, for they were impressed with both the father's and the son's conscientiousness.

'There is no better quality for people than conscientiousness; only uneducated people do not understand this.'

CXVI

Another Bird's Question for Hoopoe

The bird asked:

'Is it permissible for one to be discourteous to others? What will the outcome be if an ordinary bird is boldly blunt to an eagle that sits on a high branch of the cedar tree? Is it considered arrogant?'

CXVII

Hoopoe's Answer

Hoopoe replied:

'One should take into consideration two things when answering this question: whoever behaves discourteously before a shah should be a special person of that place. He must get rid of 'being himself' and belong to the 'other.' Then whatever words he says, it will be as if the shah spoke them. That is, 'this' and 'that' will be taken from their midst. In a way it seems daring, but it results in unity. For like the lack of one's will when he or she is in love, a lover, a beloved, drunk, or insane, so to is the blind foolishness of one how behaves with such disrespect. One should not be obstinate in their words, and should not walk in the way of arrogance or bitterness. If one's actions are comprised solely of love, he or she will have nothing to be ashamed of. Such a person will reach fullness with God and no word will pass their lips other than 'God.'"

CXVIII

A Story

There lived an ascetic with a remarkable quality. People nicknamed him 'Majnun-al-haq'.[63] For thinking of God was his passion and his mind was consumed with this night and day. If he intended to say something he always first referred to God and his answer was also given on behalf of God.

On the eve of the spring holiday he went to visit Ka'ba. He met with trouble on the road, leaving his body quite sore. The donkey he rode was also extremely weary. It became dark all around and it even began to rain. The ascetic now knew that to continue on the journey would be very difficult. He saw a ruin nearby and descended from his donkey. He left his donkey in God's care and said: 'O God, take care of my donkey!'

Leaving his donkey outside, he entered the ruin. A little later sleep began to overcome him, and so he put a piece of clay under his head and fell asleep. The voluptuous clouds of spring let down a deluge. The raindrops fell on the crazy man from every side, waking him from his repose. He got up from his place and waited in the ruin for the shower to abate. Finally, the rain subsided and the lunatic went out. He looked all about, but his donkey was not to be found! He got very upset and in his anger, yelled at God:

'I entrusted you with my donkey since you have always been good to me and have been greatly impressed by the way that you have taken care of him! Imagine what would happen, if you had guests and their donkey wandered off to the valley – they had entrusted him to your care, but you heedlessly forgot to look after it. You were embarrassed to take care of my donkey and now, in the darkness of the night you made it so that I cannot see him!'

The mystic continued to mumble angrily under his breath as he began looking low and high for his lost donkey. Just then, a bright lightning sparked and the whole landscape was filled with light. And there before his eyes was his donkey grazing. The mystic rejoiced, saddled his donkey, and continued on his way. Once he calmed down from his anger with God he became gracious and said to him:

---

[63] 'An ascetic on God's way.'

'O God, who is my soul in my body, let one hundred of my souls be sacrificed to you! Although at that time, you did not take care of my donkey or tie a rope around its neck, still, you kept it safe by hiding it. I didn't understand your plan and that is why I was impatient, and in my anger against you I went over the top. For I entrusted my donkey to you, didn't I? You were late in returning it to me. However, when you saw that I was sad, you made it all clear by striking the lightning, illuminating the eye, and lighting the fire. You revealed my donkey before my eyes and thereby expressed your grace to me.

'Although I had a right to be angry with you for what you had done, you are the one who can do the impossible, and the one who can understand difficult things. That is why you paid attention to me and found my lost item. In doing this you made me weak and ashamed of what I had said. I admit that I forgot all that you have done for me in the past. Remove these disgraces between us and acknowledge your grace. I have forgotten what happened before, and it would be good if you forgot it too. I will never put you in an awkward position again, and likewise you should also not disgrace me again. I forgave you for this event so please don't hold anything against me in your heart.'

The mystic said these words of self-praise with every breath, all the while exhibiting his bounteous affection for God. Although what the crazy man said was unpleasant in one sense, it was considered acceptable because of his love.

By this we see that if every mad person speaks secrets like these to God, they may be shameless and rude. For people like this are God's beloved and whatever a beloved person does is pleasant.

CXIX

Another Bird's Question for Hoopoe

The bird asked:
'O traveler! I am completely free from others. I am always conscious with thoughts of God and I say to myself, 'perhaps one day I will join him.' Now tell me, please, why should I travel all that way when even now I am not separated from him for a moment?'

CXX

Hoopoe's Answer

Hoopoe said to him:

'These words of yours are an empty claim. They have no connection with meaning. Nobody has ever praised himself so exaggeratedly. You should know that for months, no years, you have been going to great lengths continually praising yourself.

'You said you were surely with God, however, it does not mean that what you said is true. Really, you do not know how it would feel to be in his presence. Don't exaggerate such an empty claim. It is not clear yet whether he likes your questioning or not. He may not pay attention to what you say. You should keep respectable whatever he thinks is worth looking at. If he is not gracious and does not accept your words, then even speaking your empty speech will not be enough. It is better to wait for his grace and good works than to say these kinds of senseless words.'

CXXI

A Story

Shaikh Boyazid Bistomi was famous in the land, particularly among the erudite, for knowing things that were secrets to others and also for his refined manners. He left this world to feast in place like Paradise. One day a pupil of his saw him in his dream and asked him:

'O the only sober one among drunk people! What did the God who gives life and shows justice do for you? Let us know of your condition. We have suffered much from our separation from you, so comfort us by telling us how you are.'

The perfect mullah said to him:

'As soon as I was buried interrogating angels appeared in the grave. They asked me: 'Who is your creator and your eternal master?'

I answered:

'Do not ask me this, and if I do not answer your question don't be offended. It is better to go to him and ask him a question and see if he puts me under his authority as his servant. For, if he accepts me to be his

slave, that will serve as an answer for you. Then you must consider me to be God's slave and the slave of grace and the high throne of authority over this place. And even if he does not deprive me of being accepted, I will still be troubled by our separation. Otherwise consider me to be among the rejected and do what your heart desires!'

As soon as they heard this answer, an exclamation came from high above: 'O interrogators! He has said responsible words and by this he has proved to be our best and favorite slave.

In short, until one's eyes become filled with God's rays, to simply say something does not mean truth.

CXXII

Another Bird's Question for Hoopoe

The bird asked:

'O friend! I have become engulfed in the sea of perfection. I have reached perfection out of my greediness and my heart is satisfied with the desired goal. Since my dreams have come true here, can't you see that it would be difficult for me to endure the suffering's of a journey?'

CXXIII

Hoopoe's Answer

Hoopoe said:

'O one whose aim is despicable! Ignorance, anger, and arrogance have captured your soul. You are proud of your dream, but you are far from the real purpose. The dream you have is just vain thoughts and perhaps entirely meaningless.

'Only a flawed person will consider himself perfect. And a person who can prove his flaws is considered truly perfect by others. Those who have reached perfection don't boast about their own perfection, since this propensity exists only in flawed people.

'In terms of flaws, you have reached the highest point. You consider yourself to be a scholar when in actuality you are ignorant. To boast about one's perfection is nothing but ignorance. Therefore, if anybody considers himself to be perfect, he is sure to be flawed. For this imperfection keeps

him from being perfect.

'However, even the sun, at noon when it reaches the highest point in the sky, thinks it is perfect, but at that very moment it begins to descend, it begins to set. For the sun had true perfection, but as soon as it realizes its perfection it begins to descend.

'The imperfect man who thinks he is perfect is the same as a bad man who compares himself to a good man. It is difficult to fix this kind of person. For their house is built of pride along with arrogance.

'O weakling, you should know that when you begin to think that you are perfect, this is nothing more than imperfection itself.'

CXXIV

A Story

Shaikh Abu Bakr Nishopoori[64] was one of the people who found the way to the kingdom of meaning. One day he decided to travel about his prosperous city.

His position as Shaikh was extremely high and he had an excessive amount of devotees and servants. The people carrying his entourage and the royal banners, and the people of high class, congregated in large numbers around him. The Shaikh looked upon them with gratitude. He looked before him, behind him, and all around him, and realized that he was surrounded by people too numerous to count. Tempting thoughts came to his heart for a fleeting moment. And at that very moment a donkey brayed and let out a big fart.

Filled with delight over this, the Shaikh began a frenzied dance and then becoming faint he fell down. Seeing this, his friends and the dervishes standing about gathered around his head. When he came to his closest friend sharply asked: 'What was it?'

The Shaikh said:

'O friends who hunt for secrets! My terrible voracity attacked me as I contemplated that all the people around me were subject to me. The thought struck my inner being as I realized that of those who have been

---

[64] His real name was Abdulla ibn Muhammad and he was a famous Shaikh and law expert. He lived 853 - 935.

shown the right way – seekers, workers of good, helpers, Junaid, Shibli,[65] Boyazid, Ubaid[66], Nuri,[67] Abu Said[68] – which one of them has found prestige like mine, and on the road of poverty has been the master of such a large group of people?

'When my voracity put this thought into my heart that donkey gave the right answer. I received the needed answer from it. The reason why I was ecstatic to the point of passing out is this donkey.

'The interesting thing is that the donkey reprimanded the Shaikh to return to the right way with a bray and a fart and because it was so bizarre, he became ecstatic and the vain dreams of his head flew out like the wind.'

'Only honest people can accomplish this. If anyone is a master of honesty he will understand the meaning of this work, but no proud, mean, or loathsome person can attain this admirable state.'

CXXV

Another Bird's Question for Hoopoe

The bird asked:

'O respected one! When I take the steps of this road what deeds will make me happy? If I suffer how can I get rid of the pain? What should I do in order to know happiness in the depths of my heart and to be able to always enjoy it?'

CXXVI

Hoopoe's Answer

Hoopoe said to him:

'If you want to see yourself happy and be free of sorrow, make yourself live in a state of constant remembrance of God. If you want happiness think on him. Happiness without remembering him does not compare. It is better to have pain than to revel without him; it is one hundred times

---

[65] A great Shaikh who died in 945.

[66] A famous Shaikh.

[67] Nuri's real name was Abul-Husain Ahmad ibn Muhammad and he was a well-known Shaikh of Baghdad. He died in 907-8

[68] Abu Said Kharroz's real name was Ahmad binni Iso and he was a well-known Shaikh. He died in 899.

better to have mourning than to have a party where your mind has forgotten God. You should accept sorrow as happiness and this will free you from the manacles of evil.'

CXXVII

A Story

No wise person can explain one thousandth of what Hoja Abdulla Ansori[69] has done. He said: 'His being worthy of revelry or poverty is determined by the degree to which there was an absence of himself in his soul and the sweetheart in his memory. If any heart masters this, then consider it to be a heart. Otherwise, even if it is a sea or mine it should be given up. The heart that serves as God's abode is a heart. Otherwise, although it is a flower garden it is also a raging bonfire.

CXXVIII

Another Bird's Question for Hoopoe

The bird asked:
'O happy one! What should I request of him if I desire his love and suddenly find myself overjoyed by being united with him? I would like to know, what is the first thing that I should ask him?'

CXXIX

Hoopoe's Answer

Hoopoe said the following:
'O one with a apprehensive slogan! You have lost your reason in the valley of unrest. For he is the object of your desire and you have nobody but him. If you obtain what you need you will have embraced your beloved. Since you are far from him now, your heart will covet him and there is no other question in your heart. Likewise, if you achieve union with him and there is no separation, what more could you want? His claim is on the body and the soul and what other claim should he have? If you find

---

[69] He was a famous poet and Shaikh from Heart who lived 1005 - 1088. Alisher Nava'i held him in high regard.

him do not let your heart long for other things – give whatever you have for the sake of his love!'

CXXX

A Story

Abu Said[70] was one of the people who drowned in the river of love. The mind is too feeble to comprehend it. The nickname given to him was 'Kharroz the shoemaker' and what he did day and night was confide in God.

One day during the time of prayer in Mecca, a group of people intended to tell God what they desired. Those saintly people were aware of God's secrets and in faith beseeched him. In order for their prayers to reach God's house they rubbed their faces on the Ka'ba.

However, Abu Said, the secret of the true treasure and the beauty of the garden of union's flowers, was sad in their midst and his heart was inebriated with the goblet of unity. The people praying suddenly noticed him and the following words came to his tongue:

'O God! Whatever people have longed for I was able to reach easily. People want to find you, but as for me I have already found you. With this I look like a person who has stopped searching for you. However, I am not separated from you for a moment; to look for what is found is senseless. I have achieved my love and dream, now let these people of desire attain their goal!'

CXXXI

Another Bird's Question for Hoopoe

The bird asked:

'O knowledgeable bird! This journey damages our souls. Now if we go to the shah's feast, as its been suggested, we must take him an extremely fine gift. Tell us, what kind of gift would be suitable.'

---

[70] See footnote 63 above.

CXXXII

Hoopoe's Answer

Hoopoe said:

'You asked a very appropriate question. It would be a true labor of the heart if you took a gift to him. It needs to be priceless, perhaps decorated with rubies, and more costly than pure pearl.

However, there are many precious things in his treasury that will make pure pearl inconsequential. By precious things I mean the prayers and righteousness of angels and those whose lusts are to keep themselves pure. Many prayers uttered by eremites can be found there. The pearls of righteousness and prayer can be found in abundance in that place, as well as difficulties endured by prophets, and the prayers of saints. What deserves praise here is considered equal with dirt there.

'There the best gift is to burn and endure maladies. There is no better gift than a sigh of grief. For that place is the house of respect and peace and it is more excellent than one hundred regions of a thousand paradises. Of greatness, strength, and coquetry there is more than enough. Displays of weakness and begging cannot be found there.

'Take pleading and malady with you and bring your needy body and sorrowful soul because these gifts are not available in that place. Ask the shah to accept them as you come powerless and weak. If you want to become his companion go before him consumed by woe and nothingness.'

CXXXIII

A Story

There lived a king who was the shah of shahs. His presence was like the shadow of God in the world. He had a crown that was as bright as the sun and the pearls that decorated it shone like stars. His wealth stretched from east to west.

He also had a son. The world has yet to see again such a gallant son. It is not enough to compare his handsomeness with a bright star in the sky or a glittering pearl of a jewelry box. He was the glowing candle of beauty's night and the beautiful cypress of the flower garden.

Since the shah thought that such beauty should not pass before the

people of the world, he kept him concealed in a castle. He did this because he thought that his son's beauty would cause upheaval. He also would block any road that his son would ride out on. Like a peacock the son would relax and stroll though the gardens. Since the shah forbid him to go out beyond their grounds, he spent his time enjoying himself there. Then one day the shah died and left his throne to the prince. The government proclaimed the glory of his name and stamped it onto the coins.

One day to cheer himself in his grief, he rode around to view his country. With long strides he entered the square. Galloping now upon his horse, he played polo,[71] and as the people bowed their heads he took their lives. Wherever he went the people let out a great shout and loud clamor. Upon sight of him, people went mad and were stricken with love.

Like a wind that sweeps through the land, leaving in its wake a path of destruction, the prince quickly returned to his flower garden. The people of city cried out before him 'O, Lord!' Their cries and sighs of love reached even to the heavens. They did not stay in the city but followed him to his castle and garden.

The afflicted ones destroyed his property and swarmed his castle. The crowd was warned: 'Those who have started this uprising will be exiled and those who do not leave will be punished!'

No matter how hard the shah's officers tried to disperse the crowd they refused to leave. All the officers' attempts were in vain. The people of the city were crazy, they were more than crazy, and day and night they staked themselves around the shah's garden. Both young and old, drunkards and eremites, people of high and low position—all the crowds had taken to the road of love and senselessness.

When the shah saw the affected state of the people he was shocked. He saw that this madness had no end and understood that there was no way of solving it. He sent a messenger to the people with this order: 'the ones who are captive to my love all have work to do. Let them do their best to show that they are skilled in their field. Everybody must be occupied with his or her trade. If I like anybody's work then they will become aware of me and I will appoint them to be my ministers. They will be my companions during feasts, in conversation, and travel. But if I do not like their work let them be beheaded and die a painful death!' It was the decree of the shah

---

[71] In the Central Asian way of polo the head of a sheep is used as the ball.

whose duty it was to bring people under control.

The lovers had to withstand the test. People were hopeful of attaining his promise and began to fulfill their duty. All professors, scholars, and craftsmen forgot everything else and restlessly tried to do what the shah had ordered. Scholars wanted to write books and musicians wanted to compose new songs. Poets tried to write verses that would be worthy for the shah to look at. Scribes tried to write a letter that the shah would notice, they took their pencil and began to describe him. A jeweler tried to create a golden belt to match him. A tailor went to his workroom and began to make a brocaded robe for the shah to wear. A carpenter made a throne for the shah hoping he would enjoy sitting on it. A bow maker prepared a bow and was busy with its artwork. In order to please the shah, an arrow maker made some arrows that required intricate work.

In short, everybody in the city was occupied with their work, hoping that the shah would accept it and invite him or her to be his minister. They wanted the shah to be pleased with the result of their labor and so accomplish their goal.

One night the shah came out of his castle to see what the people were up to. One or two of his guardians accompanied him and with the instincts of thieves kept him from being seen. One by one his eyes saw everything his people were doing. The great shah remarked to himself: 'we have this and more in our treasury.'

He walked and walked and at last came to a house where a poor man lived. This man was in love, suffered greatly, and had become weak. His soul was hopelessly in love and the feeling of separation from the one he loved depressed him. The blood that was beating out of his heart dripped from his eyes. The dripping blood covered the floor and the distress of his heart tortured him like a bird half slaughtered. At every moment he suffered and people's hearts were broken by his sighs and cries. The dagger of love had stabbed his heart and his life was slowly seeping out of this wound. Since he was so tormented by love he was near nonexistence. This nothingness accompanied him to the ground and as he laid there every hair of his body felt intense pain.

He said to himself:

'Everybody is lovingly show-casing their specialty. Tomorrow they will participate in the shah's feast and he will express his gratitude to each one of them. Yet I have nothing but a piece of grief and sorrow to present him. How can I accompany them tomorrow?'

'The shah either loves or despises. Oh, I hope he allows me go to his palace despite my poverty. However, I do not deserve his kindness and I do not even deserve for him to take the time to despise me. It would be enough glory for me if he quarreled with me and then beheaded me with his sword. I have no other goal. However, I am not worth consideration and I am not even sure he will condescend to kill me. Oh, my anguish is increasing to the point that it endangers my very life and I'm now mourning it!'

Seeing the state of this poor man the shah's heart melted and like the sun he entered the destitute house. The shah was pleased with him, his heart burned and he thought his spirit had left his body. Seeing this, the poor lover was rendered deaf and dumb. His heart could not contain such joy and so he presented his life to the guest before him.

'You should know that to die like this is better than life. It is worth more than one thousand lives. If a man has a chance to die this way, but does not leave his life he is not a man. To suffer and burn of love turns the soul's candlelight into a torch. As the suffering candle's tears, produced by the heat of the flame, fall down its side; it replaces the sun in the dark night.'

"O Foni[72]! If you want to find the way make yourself happy with sighing, burning, and ailing!"

CXXXIV

Another Bird's Question for Hoopoe

The bird asked:
'O bird that knows the way of purity and guidance! The intensities of this way have been more than enough and the end has not limit. Tell me, please, when are we going to pass over this wasteland of evil? How do we reach the true place? Give us the details of the work ahead, of the restful and the strenuous junctures of the route. How does it start and with what does it end? First tell of the difficulties we will encounter and then about its purpose and pleasure.

---

[72] 'Foni' means 'nothingness'. Nava'i uses it as his pen name.

CXXXV

Hoopoe's Answer

Hoopoe said the following:

'O companion of the road! You ask a delicate question. You want to know about this journey, its difficulties and joys. At the offset, you should know that this route consists of several valleys and destinations. Let me comment on them one by one and you will be informed.

'Before us lie seven large valleys. Each of them has more than enough peril. They consist of innumerable destinations and one cannot count them all. However, all these destinations lead to seven large valleys.

'First is the Valley of Seeking and only the one who can show the right way may lead to it.

'Next is the Valley of Love. Here everything that you have and don't have must be put on fire.

'Once love burns up your existence the Valley of Enlightenment appears

'Then comes the Valley of Needlessness. It is extremely wide and the high sky lies low before it.

'After that is the Valley of Oneness. To cross this valley one must be alone.

'When you pass that valley, you encounter the Valley of Bewilderment. It is intense.

'After everything is the Valley of Poverty and Nothingness The travelers who are spiritually pure will finish here. They will attain their goal in different ways.

'However, nobody has ever sent a message back from these destinations or has returned after leaving. There are many unknowns and uncertainties in identifying these seven valleys.'

CXXXVI

The Valley of Seeking

'If you go into the Valley of Seeking you will face thousands of sorrows and griefs at every moment. With every breath you will feel one hundred hardships and your being will change one thousand times. The torture of

desire will distress your heart and the inability to find anything will ravage your spirit.

'With this will come the determined deprivation of your soul and union with the beloved will be uncertain. Difficulties and disasters will thrust into your body and powerful illnesses will break it. You will want to have a very rare pearl, but you won't able to find it. It will be necessary to give up the tools of this world to obtain it.

'Sufis must give up their wealth and whatever obscures the way and in a loud voice praise the four ways of nothingness. They must lead themselves to the destination of the goal throwing away everything except their eagerness for the way.

'If nothing of the world's material remains new qualities will appear in you. From this treasure prosperity will come to your ruin and heavenly light will brighten your soul. This light will flame your desire day by day and make your horse of seeking swift. Instead of one quests you will find one hundred quests. At that time mountains will be rolling hills to you. Your heart will feel the ease of seeking and the vehemence of enduring difficulties will free you. The more you want to find pearls the easier it will be to be a diver. When union's sun shows its face your dusk will mingle with your dawn. If a drunken elephant comes up to you, you will not even consider it to be a fly. If one hundred lions stand in your way, you will see them as lame ants. If you get to the treasure even a dragon will not be dangerous for you. If you wash your hands of infidelity and religion a door will open before you. When you enter neither infidelity nor religion will be inside and you will forget all of it. For neither infidelity nor religion is appropriate for a person who is on this journey. They are just obstacles in the real way.'

CXXXVII

A Story

There lived a powerful king. His wealth, like his soldiers were innumerable. He had a handsome son and even Joseph's beauty was nothing in comparison. The Eastern sun would completely bow before his beauty since it was embarrassed. The cypress was ready to shade the tender shoot and the moon was ready to reflect his sun-like face. Like the

sun his beauty was a world conqueror and like the moon his face was a king who radiated. The world would be harmed whenever he looked at it and would make the lovers love the other world. When his lips started speaking souls were taken and when he smiled life was revived.

The whole world was in love with him and if he killed them they would not care. His infidel and drunken eyes always killed believers and religious people. He rode his sparking horse like lightning in every direction, and the world was on fire. The whole world was fascinated with him but he was too enchanting for them. If he looked at people out of the corner of his eye thousands would bleed from the sword of his tyranny. He was not worried about the destruction of the world's nations, but would kill them with his despotism. Even the wind was afraid of blowing on his street and since it was not able to blow in his garden his flowers belittled it.

One day he decided to ride around the ranges of his steppe. Thousands of dervishes were lying there and all of them did not know what to do with the intensity of their love for him. They did not have a chance to look at his face and it was no use looking in that direction. Everybody, good or bad, wanted to see his face but it was impossible.

Suddenly the happy prince saw two weak lovers who were in a chain of love. The prince ordered his servants: 'Bring these two dervish looking people to me'. They grabbed the two afflicted ones and rode toward the king's castle. The king put one of them in a dungeon and appointed the second one as the caretaker of his dog. The first one joined the prisoners in the dungeon and the second one was chained to dogs. For a long time they suffered like this.

An ill person asked each of them:

'How do you handle this suffering?'

The dog caretaker said:

'Is it suffering? Isn't it pleasure! Where is the suffering you see? My heart is satisfied with his love and I am ready to be a dog in his street. Although I am his dogs servant I am their leader.'

The prisoner said:

'If his love was too powerful for my heart I would be ready to lie down in my grave. Although I am chained in the dungeon my heart has hope from his love.'

The king with moon-like beauty was listening to what they said from a hidden place. They were faithful to their desire and deserved love. The shah

was endlessly happy like the sun and enjoyed their words very much.

He showed them great interest and made them his closest aides. This is the result of their faithfulness to their seeking.

CXXXVIII

The Valley of Love

'Once you cross the Valley of Seeking then you enter the Valley of Love.

'Love is a torch that does not extinguish. Do not call it a torch; call it a spark that lights the whole world. Not everybody deserves love. What creature except a Salamander can move in fire? Courage and poverty are needed to love and one must be a Salamander in the sea of fire. To be a lover means to burn in the flame like a moth. Don't say the work of beauties is wisdom; a butterfly does not deserve to be a moth. A butterfly flies among the flowers showing children its beauty and elegance. However, it cannot do what dervishes who wear tattered clothes can do. Can the butterfly fly into the flame like a moth? Although a butterfly is seen as beautiful with its many colors and dots, it cannot burn like a moth. Can a bird that does not burn with love be called a nightingale?

'If anyone does not burn in love it means he is not in love. Whoever does not sacrifice his life; do not consider him to be a lover. People who are in love are happy to suffer and burn, but love is not reached just by suffering. The fire that comes out of the lover's heart is powerful like the dragon's fire that can burn down a building.

'The lover's soul is no stranger to fervent sighs. What else comes out of the fire pit except smoke? The fire of love can burn the whole world like lightning. Only a true lover may suffer of love and his pain looks like lightning on a haystack.

'Do not say that the lover does not like fire, but it is love that made his heart into a fire temple. And if he falls into the fire there is no other way than to burn.

'If anybody turns into a fire of love, do not be surprised, because whatever falls into the fire will light into fire. Love covers a lover's body like fire covers the one who walks close to it.

'You cannot play with love. If it comes to your body, it will make

you roam like a sandstorm. In love one must suffer and in the fire there is no other way but to burn. The moment lightning flashes in love's sky the fire will take one's soul into its realm. The lightning of love will burn everything; the whole world will be on fire!

'You should know that the lover's main work is to leave his life. To die for a soul mate should not be hard to do.'

CXXXIX

A Story

On his way to the Hajj, Asma'iy[73] saw trees and flowers growing at a rest stop. A brook was running down the middle of a field of green grass and a flower garden. It was a sign of life. The ditch was as clean and pure as a lover's soul, and pure water flowed like lover's tears.

Asma'iy sat by the soothing water for a while to rest and get rid of his deep sorrows. As he settled in his eyes caught the sight of an inscribed stone at the head of the brook. It said: 'O hajj going people, find the way to disclose this secret. What should one do if he is afflicted with love and it has taken his patience away?'

Asma'iy took a pen and an ink bottle and wrote the following under the inscription: 'Whoever has fallen into this dangerous vortex and wants to come out of it pure, he should not be afraid of his present way.' After he wrote this answer he left that place. The next day he returned and looked at the inscription on the stone again. The previous scribe had now written the following: 'What should he do when the wounded lover's soul is pure and he keeps his love in secret, but the love he has in his heart is so intense that he is short-tempered and needs to see his sweetheart? What should he do if he cannot find the way out of it?'

When Asma'iy saw this extraordinary secret he wrote with his mystical pen: 'If a person who is in love is too sick and weak to reach the goal of my advice, he should die and get rid of love.' Having written this deadly answer the cruel counselor left the brook quickly. The next day he was delayed somewhere else and then rode his camel back to see what the anonymous sad lover answered. When he arrived he saw a person lying

---

[73] Asma'iy was a well-known Arabic linguist. His full name was Abu Said Abdumalik binni Quraib. He died in 828.

near the brook who looked depressed and had given up on life. He had a sickly face and was a spiritless person who could wreck people's heart with his condition. He had solved the perplexity of being in love by bashing his head onto a stone. When his head struck, the stone broke. His blood made the brook flow red as his head laid on the stone beside the water. On account of the advice given, the lover had given up his soul and became free of the suffering of unrequited love.

When Asma'iy saw this unusual event he felt jabbed by a hundred stingers. He tore his robe, threw down his turban and mourned for the person who had followed his advice. Since he had never seen a more powerful event he wailed and wept bitterly. His heart grieved what had been done; he dug the ground and placed the dead one in the tomb. Since the deceased man was a martyr his bloody clothes served as the burial cloth.

"O Foni! This is the way of being nothing in love. If you are not patient, surrender your soul just like this. Whoever is granted this kind of death by God is worth my sacrificing one hundred thousand lives of mine!"

CXL

The Valley of Enlightenment

'You should know that after the Valley of Love is the Valley of Enlightenment. Gaze your eyes on it; it consists of a wasteland without borders.

'Whoever enters this valley will see contradictions here. Roads numbering one hundred thousand cross it, but not one of them look alike. Differences and oppositions between the whole and a part exist here as well. There is development and also decay. You can see one hundred thousand anxious travelers and all of them go their own way. Each one is proud of their chosen way and they are bent towards their own way. The road dear to one is not wanted by another. Everybody likes his road and ignores the other's.

'The flea and the elephant are travelers here and both Gabriel and the flea fly. Moses and Pharaoh are also travelers here, however, you should know that these two are not the same. Both Mahdiy[74] and Dajjol[75] cannot

---

[74] Mahdiy was the last prophet of the twelve prophets. He has disappeared and will appear on Judgment Day to fight against Dajjol whom he is destined to slaughter.

[75] A wild creature.

be compared with the mule that Jesus rode on the road. Muhammad and Abu Jahl[76] can also be seen there. One fell into darkness and the other drowned in light.

'All bad and good people walk here. Both Muslim and infidel are travelers here. Fire worshippers move towards their idols, and the people of Ka'ba worship one God. Infidels call upon idols but Muslims repeat, 'Allah is one.'[77]

'It is impossible for anything to be without contradiction here, because the roads themselves cross each other. The prophet guide has said: 'Whoever wants to find God should go on the journey and see that it consists of many roads whose number can be compared to the breaths of the people.' All of these roads are not dirty and they are all not clean either. In religions these contradictions are sure to exist. It is necessary.

'The beggar and the king accomplish enlightenment in their own way. It is good if one attempts this, as one should obtain knowledge and perfection. There will be a difference in this way if one religious person puts their head on the prayer mat and the other worships an idol. What one knows will be characteristic of him. Enlightenment makes these kinds of distinctions. Every person strives in their sphere and walks in this valley.

'Although there are various changes in the method, all who enter in this way have the same goal. On this road, whether it is crooked or straight, far or near, whether some will die, get lost or just roam the paths, it is impossible to reach the goal if one is not moving.

'When the sun of enlightenment shows its face everybody will want the results of their spiritual striving and obtain concrete wealth. For when the pure ray streams forth it will light the way for those who try to be perfect. Whoever suffers difficulties on the way will have treasure at the end of his journey. There are a lot of contrasts in the way, most of them are dirty, and the pure ones are few. Those who submit to the prophet's rules of Shari'at will be owners of pure nature.'

---

[76] A man who fought against Muhammad. He symbolizes cruelty and ignorance.
[77] 'Illalloh' in Arabic.

CXLI

A Story

Listen! This incident may serve you as a good example. They say a group of blind people was either roaming or captive in India. And as fate would have it they somehow returned again to their country. Someone asked them: 'Did you see an elephant?'

'Yes, we did', they answered.

'If you have seen the elephant, tell us about it', said the person.

Actually they did not see an elephant and they did not even really inquire about it either. However, each one of them had touched different parts of the elephant and so had some knowledge about it. Therefore, the one who felt the elephant's legs said it looked like a pillar, and the one who touched the elephant's stomach said that it did not look like a pillar, but a mountain.[78] The one who held his trunk said it resembled something of a dragon. The one who was informed of its teeth said that the elephant consisted of two bones. The one who was enlightened about the elephant's tail compared it to a dangling snake. The one who touched the elephant's head explained that it was the top of a peak. And the one who felt the elephant's ears said that it was two wafting fans.

All of them spoke like this since they were blind. Although what they said was correct it had some flaws. It did not have any order.

That is why a leading philosopher who was a master in the field of elephants and had Indian ancestors listened and did not reprimand anybody but said:

'These blind men all shared what they knew about elephants. Although they each made contradictory statements they can be forgiven. For each spoke from what he knew, however, not one of them saw the elephant. But if you put everything that they said in order you will have a definite picture of what an elephant is.'

'Since it is clear for one who can envision, he can accept everything that the blind say to be true.'

CXLII

The Valley of Needlessness

'Next is the Valley of Needlessness where people of high and low class are equal.

'The wind of the Valley of Needlessness is swift and disturbs the world. The one hundred thousand worlds will be swept away by the pouring rain of its clouds. It is small like a raindrop in seven seas or a poppy seed in seven skies. If the fire of seven hells is only equal to a spark before this lightning, then eight paradises are just dew.

'Here ants feed on lions and fleas are capable of hunting elephants. The heroic shah who was able to conquer seven countries is equal to a simple beggar. The blade of execution with its army of one hundred stands at attention. Nobody cares about the expensive clothes made even from martens. The Dragon that is able to swallow the whole sky is equal to Saint Mary's fine thread there. Angel flocks by the thousands were neglected and suddenly Adam wore the glorious crown. When a hundred thousand spirits lost their body, Noah saved the lives of people from disaster by shipbuilding.

'Everybody is equal there including: Nimrod[79] who has been bitten by innumerous flies and Halil who turned fire into a flower. Or the one hundred thousand innocent children whose blood has been shed praising God's Word, or the hundreds of thousands who gave up their religion and those wearing the Christian belt whose souls have found comfort in Christ's breath. Or the old tyrant who shed the blood of one hundred thousand people, and Muhammad's travel to the top of Heaven one night. Everything that exists or does not exist, both religious people and infidels is equal there.

'If Zakhkhok[80] shed people's blood for one thousand years and Christ gave life to a dead body, or Bukhtunnasr[81] was vengeful and Nooshiravon[82]

---

[78] 'Bisutun.' In Uzbek this word has two meanings, 'mountain' and 'without pillars'.

[80] According to Persian history Zakhkhok was a cruel shah with a snake on his shoulder.

[81] Bukhtunnasr was a destructive shah.

[82] Nooshiravon (Anooshirvon) was a nickname of an Iranian shah who belonged to the Sasonids dynasty. His real name was Khusrav ibn Qubod. He lived 531-589. He symbolizes the just shah in Oriental literature.

was just, the two are seen as the same. See what needlessness looks like!

'If one hundred thousand suns vanish consider it a particle in the sky. Even if one hundred thousand deep seas get absorbed consider it a drop. If one hundred thousand beautiful fairies burn and turn into ash, consider it the broken wing of one fly. If the wind blows away nine layers of the heavens, consider it to be blown chaff. Compare the lost of the huge mountain Qof with the lost of a grain of sand. If cedars and trees of Paradise vanish the forest is less a leaf. That is all.

'The strayed and the vigilant are equal there. The wine house and God's house are the same there. Whether the fire worshipper's faith is high or low Ka'ba and the idol house are considered equal. A one thousand year old elephant is equal to a baby elephant born this morning and this enormous world equal to a piece of a small poppy seed. The number of infidels and religious people are the same there, and the believer will face many difficulties.'

CXLIII

A Story

Two chess masters opened the chessboard sat on opposite sides and poured out the big chess pieces.[83] On both sides there was a king who was placed in his place of honor and they had real servants and warriors. Each of them had advisors to go straight and a queen to go roundabout. One of the kings was of the white Romans, the other one was shah of the dark people. The masters lined up their kings and the other decorated pieces on the board.

Then the opponents rode onto the board and enthusiastically deployed various tactics. It looked like a fortress surrounded by a battlefield. One side was eager to defeat the other. The war lines contained elephants, giraffes, bears, and castles. The infantry tried to fight swiftly before the cavalry.

The armies battled each other using various tactics in accordance with the rules of war. If one side hid his army in ambush the other side

---

[83] As seen in this detailed story about chess, Nava'i loved chess.

tried to break it up. The play in the middle was amazing. They showed immeasurable guile and war strategy. Both commanders and brave fighters attacked each other. As the two heroic shahs mapped out their forces it looked as if they were about to fight to the death. The battle was fierce with outstanding armies, noise, fortresses, fields, and cavalry. There were victorious assaults and there were retreats in the left flanks and the right flanks.

The son of each commander went to the fore of the battle and started fighting before their father. After crossing over the field they replaced their father. A soldier came from one side and quickly changed the outlook by his heroism on the field. All by himself he could repel a whole army.

The battlefield was full of such coincidences, as if two enraged shahs were fighting each other and had young men who were born to fight. However, this kind of battlefield is rarely encountered. Wars are not so quick and the people so well armed.

The building up of forces, the field, having mutual enemies and the regulations of war - all of it would fall down and be nothing if anyone decides to gather the player pieces and pick up the chessboard. Not a trace of warfare, enmity, or the rules of war would remain. All that has happened and the customs; that is the attacks of the two sides on the battlefield is nothing for the person who carefully thinks it over. Like a maid who is one hundred years old, they are worth nothing. For they can both be wrapped in a piece of burlap and thrown into fire or water.

When the game ends, it will make no difference for the master who played the game. Look at the chess pieces that are put inside a small sack. The king may fall to the bottom and infantry be on top of him.

They are the mark of needlessness. Finally, look at this example and know one hundred thousand times better than real needlessness. If you find the meaning of this way, compare all works with it!

CXLIV

The Valley of Oneness

'You should know that after this is the Valley of Oneness. Understand that you must be alone there and without surplus.

'If you want to travel in this valley, the main regulation for you will be

solitariness. When your travel finally comes to an end you will consider one hundred birds to be one bird. All of their aims are oneness and so all their songs and melodies will be of oneness. If hermits reach this state, it will be their main effort to loose themselves in oneness. For one times one equals one and reason will not dare grasp it.

'If this difficult work obstructs you then remember that everything is nothing except oneness. Be one, see one, say one and desire one! Never wish for two. For two is surplus on this journey and will prevent you from understanding the secrets of oneness.'

CXLV

A Story

Mansur achieved much in oneness, and used to continually repeat, 'I am truth.'[84]

Religious people would tell him that this was not a good thing to do and that it was shaming to his friends and relatives. Although most of the supporters of Sufism knew it too, they remained disciplined in their state. You too should behave as they did and not make such a claim, so that your passions don't deserve the gallows' rope. As the wine that inebriated him was so strong he did not cease from repeating that melodious line.

One day he was in a funny mood and began thinking of all kinds of things. His thoughts went to the prophet of Allah. He saw Muhammad riding his horse called Buroq in the sky and granted him a crown made of the pearl of oneness. A staircase of oneness was his ladder with the high sky as close as two eyebrows and he reached closeness with purity and appealed to God who had said to him: 'O friend, what is your desired intention?' There he begged God's forgiveness, as he desired for the sins of his guilty community to be forgiven. He had enough alms and graces for all. He had more than enough grace for his people and he was generous. Even God himself wanted it and showed him limitless kindness. With this the shah of Arabs requested the forgiveness of sins for his guilty community. Whoever has traveled on the crooked path from the first day to eternity, his mercy is sufficient. He told God that he should not withhold charity

---

[84] His words were "Anal-haq" which literally means " I am truth" and implies "I am God". Mansur Al Hallaj (858-922) was hung for these words by the religious leaders.

and forgive those who have passed away. Why was he satisfied with only asking God for people's sins to be forgiven considering their loyalty and purity?

These thoughts came to Mansur's mind and he always remembered them. This submission exasperated him and he was surprised to not know anything about it. One day in his dream the prophet of Allah enlightened him. He said the following and Mansur was solved of his problems:

'O one who sits in the dullness of the porch and in the name of oneness likes to repeat: 'I am truth!' Didn't you know that when I was riding in the heavens that night there was no thought of 'myself'; maybe there is no need to say this word. For it was he who led, who carried, who desired that place and only he who devoted himself.

'Since you can't see far away, you let us know that you are blind, and ignorant. For in the Valley of Oneness with your garden of singleness and loneliness you opened up the direction of "me" and "you". However, the valley had been free of this kind of duality. It is he who said it, who gave it, who presented it and who dispersed it and picked it! That composition was purer than the color of your 'selfishness', and there was no dissonance in its tune.

'I thought of your 'selfishness' and thought two things. Your state is nothing but being cross-eyed, that is, you cannot look in the same direction at once. You see one thing as two. Throw this thought away as nothing.'

CXLVI

The Valley of Bewilderment

'When you cross the Valley of Oneness, you will undoubtedly see the Valley of Bewilderment. Here a person will have a thousand sighs and one hundred thousand regrets as a sword's edge does not reach all the way to his head. Bewilderment makes the tongue dumb. A person will not know if it is day or night, or whether he exists or not, or what will happen tomorrow. Everything he sees will shock him and in his shock he will roam around in futility.

'Whenever the travelers take a step they have nothing but surprises.

Hallaj (858-922) was hung for these words by the religious leaders.

Whatever he achieved in the previous valleys is nothing here. He forgets about his life. He will not be able to answer if he is asked about his existence. He doesn't know whether he is in the middle, on one side, outside, in the corner, or standing in front. Surprise keeps him from all of them.

'He doesn't understand if he lives in nothingness or forever and if he is drunk or sober. He doesn't know whether he exists or not, whether his kind is known or unknown. Wherever he looks he sees unending surprise and is overwhelmed. Once he said to himself that he was in love but he did not know with whom he had fallen in love. He will be immersed in bafflement by looking into a speck of dust through specks of dust and trying to confirm if they exist or not. These things happen very often in this place and one surprise will not even be finished with when another thousand come.'

CXLVII

A Story

There lived a king who conquered the world. Hundreds of sultans used to bow in his house. His wealth was more than more and everything was under his decree.

He had a pearl that he tried to hide from everybody. The beauty of girls and fairies were embarrassed before this beauty. She was a young and tender shoot in the garden of beauty. She was not only a tender shoot she was the exalted one of the beauties. She was a life-giving candle. No, not a candle, but like the torch of the bright sun. The well of her winking eyes would kill you and the world has still not seen such disastrous eyes. Her hair curls and beauty mark were the scent of excitement and nobody who met her could remain unscathed. Her red lips pleased and spoke very beautifully. They could be compared with Christ and the sun. Hoping for her love, many rich people and grand shah's tried, but did not succeed and not one of their hearts was happy with her. This beautiful woman did not want to be close with people. The two sides were not eager to be close: that is, who can be a mate with one who is singular in the whole world? If this is how she was, who else would want to have taken her?

One night this beautiful woman had a vision. A handsome young man

disturbed her heart. His spirit was pure and clean. On his face was written a letter with fragrant musk and his beauty mark was the dot of that letter. His cruelty and handsomeness was a cypress and his tenderness and beauty a flower. If this boy was the lamp of the sun, the woman was the full moon that radiated him. The two of them sat on a throne and drank constantly of union's goblet with great pleasure.

The flower face opened her eyes from her slumber but wished to go back. Her resolve was gone. With every breath her love increased and she realized that she was in trouble. She kept seeing this same dream but tears did not let her eyes have sleep. Now day and night she did not know what peace was, as hers was broken and rest was gone.

One day the pain was too much and she went up to her high tower. To give peace to her heart she looked in all directions and tried to be calm. Suddenly, while she was letting out a burning sigh, she caught sight of the shah's feast. There she saw the man of her dreams and sighing again she fainted. The young man she saw was the youngest of the shah's servants and was the one who made the world suffer.

At that moment the young man looked in the direction of the woman and his heart immediately became the target of love. His weak heart became anxious and it afflicted his body. There was an insurrection in his heart that threatened to assassinate it. He did not have patience or consciousness but had left with them.

It continued this way till evening. He did not know whether he was dead or alive. When it grew dark and he was covered in a shroud he began groaning. The tears of wailing that dropped from his eyes looked like a typhoon. When the morning bird revealed the previous night's secrets, the young man spent his day from early till late beating his chest with a stone.

Love made the two sides suffer this way. It was as if love was thrashing about in two different countries. Although the young man felt weak with love for the woman, he kept himself using a lot of magic. However, the moon-like beauty was becoming extremely weak of love and was starting to give up. She saw that her hope was leaving her and that it looked like it was going to end tragically. Therefore, there was no way but to search for a way out because her love could not stay hidden.

She had two close attendants who always helped her in happy and sorrowful times. They were masters of finding solutions, and skillful magicians. They were so cunning and learned in their craft that they could

even make a fly and an elephant into a couple. They did it so well that the fly would not feel small nor the elephant think that his body was huge. Each of them was a master of such trickery and deception and they could do battle with love as well.

One of them was a skilled player of a stringed musical instrument and the second one was a singer. They played the instrument and sang wonderfully and the music they played went up into the sky to make its home in Venus. If one of them took a person's soul by her singing, the second one brought it back by her playing. When wise people would hear them they would lose their consciousness.

When the moon-like beauty's love pains increased she called her two attendants to an isolated place. Weeping bitterly she told them everything that had happened to her. She then said:

'You are my beloved friends. Help me to be free of this situation. Otherwise my secret's thorn will blossom and the people will see it. The fire of this love will burn my body and turn it into ashes. However, I am not afraid of suffering and if I die I won't be sorry. I exaggerated in my praying, and now if people find out my secret I will die of shame! I worry that my father will suffer shame from it. I don't know how to explain it, because this one person's disgrace would be a great shame for the shah of the sky. It means nothing to my father if one hundred girls like me die, like a straw that sank into the sea. I cannot endure a great shah, like my father, being shamed, and so my problems are rising.

'I told you what happened to me and now it is up to you what to do. Either kill me or find the way out of it! If I was restive before, now I am weak in love's grasp. If I was powerful before, now I am feeble. Have mercy on my pitiful situation and understand my sorrow!'

When the two heard this they gave themselves to the princess and said:

'Let us find the answer. That handsome young man should be your closest companion! Let no one know what we are about to do. May not even that young man sense it. However, you have to be patient for some days, and stop from groaning at every moment. For your want it to be done secretly and that is how we intend to do it.'

The moon-like beauty decided to be patient in the hope of seeing him.

The two wise attendants pondered carefully, started their plan and met the young man often. They made him their friend and saw that his heart

felt the same. They used so much magic and craftiness that the poor young man was under their spell. One of them became his mother and the second one was his sister.

They said to the young man: 'We will find a solution for you. Although you have not made your situation known to us, we are aware of it. If her love crushed your heart we have the answer of union for your separation!'

These words made him happy and he listened to them intently. Whatever the two ordered him to do he fulfilled it with pleasure. Using their armory of craftiness and trickery, the young bird was hunted.

They invited him to their place and that poor boy went to their place happily. They put together a regal feast there that was pleasing to the soul. He, who was love's captive started to drink the wine. When the wine took effect, he began telling various stories from his life. He spoke about fire and the smoke of his love, the use and harm of union and separation, and the attendants told him secrets which interested him and commented to him on a lot things. Hearing it the hopeless man attained his goal, just like the goblet he had drunk.

After drinking the wine and a long conversation, the young man became deaf and dumb with love and suddenly began to feel weak. Then they took a stringed musical instrument and began playing a captivating song. The weak one listened to the song and fainted as if from wine.

The night was black without limits. The fainted young man lay before the shrewd attendants and they did what they had set out to do. They were not passive in their work but with vigor they made a large box. They put him into the box and quickly took him to the moon-like beauty's feast. There every instrument was ready to make it enjoyable and a sweet-lipped woman was waiting for them in a hidden place. The two clever attendants brought that white-bodied cypress to her throne. His was given to the owner of the throne. The moon had found the sun.

With the union, she ordered his face to be sprinkled with perfume. When the scent of roses brought him back to life, he opened his eyes and saw a place like Paradise. Beside him was a beautiful woman who looked like a fairy and who made his heart race. He jumped up and in his excited state had to sit back down. He started to look around in surprise. Below him was the grand shah's throne and beside him was a smiling attractive woman. Then he said to himself: 'O Lord! What is this? Is it my dream, my reality or my imagination?'

The moon-like woman soothed him saying sweet words and while fulfilling the rituals of union said: 'O one who lost consciousness, this is not a dream. Give thanks, and now drink from the goblet of union.' The fairy took the goblet and drank it. She then filled the cup again and passed it to him.

The beautiful cup-bearer, who wore fine clothes gave the young man many cups to drink. When the wine goblet extinguished the fire of shame, they openly began speaking words of love to each other. The sorrowful lovers were together in the house of dissipation. They achieved such oneness that there was no notion of duality. They went as far as their desire allowed. They found everything they wanted from each other. They were so indulging that it would not be right to describe what they did. They were thirsty and needy, their face and mouth was on the other's. The rest that they did can be compared with this. One can guess what it ended with. They both played out indulging acts and were busy with such revelry till the morning.

The morning revealed the night's secrets and the white thing began to sprinkle on darkness like musk on the ground. The dawn was getting light. The wine had had a strong effect on them and they were very weak. Being concerned about it the two attendants stood by the curtain and began playing a song. They stole the minds of the feast participants and made the young man unconscious again. After the cunning attendants managed this, they tightly tied his feet and put him back into the box and took him back to where they got him in the first place. They took the one who suffered of love to his house of sorrow.

When the boy came to, the early morning breeze touched his nose. He opened his eye and began wondering. The past events were reenacted in his mind one by one. Remembering his sweetheart, he let out a sad wail from within. He hit his whole body with rocks and there was no spot that was not bruised. He was in great crisis and this bright world became dark to his eyes. Tears fell from his eyes like the stars as he groaned and then shouted at the walls.

Thinking of the uniting feast, he cried like a crazed man.

'O God! What am I to do? Who can I talk to about my state? If I don't tell anyone, will I not remain sad? Will I not lose my patience? What if I cannot find the strength to be calm? I do not know if I should keep my situation hidden or make it known, I do not know if I should speak or stay

silent! It is not possible to speak even one thousandth of it. If I think of hiding it, I might die.'

He had no power in his body or consciousness in his head. His shock inflicted his heart at every moment and people were surprised at his state as well. If anybody asked him about his well-being he would not answer but only said: 'Don't ask me about it, it is enough for me to burn from it, please do not make me burn more. I can't comment anymore and you cannot know it until you have it.'

'O God! Who was that person who achieved success at the feast of union, wasn't it me? If I were to describe it, would others believe it? What am I to do, the shock is killing my heart! What am I to do, she is killing my ruined body! At first I achieved the goal of union and copulated with my sweetheart. Then I encountered separation and now I am immersed in shock. O God! I am in a very horrible predicament. Do not let anyone else be in such.'

CXLVIII

The Valley of Poverty and Nothingness

When you pass the Valley of Bewilderment you will come across the Valley of Poverty and Nothingness. There is nothing but sadness, dumbness, deafness and unconsciousness in this valley. For it is in the vortex of the typhoon, and one hundred thousand worlds can sink in it. The strong storm forms thousands of patterns with its high waves. These patterns often disappear and numerous new waves appear again. If you look at this phenomenon closely you will see the absence of substance in the waves, because everything but the sea itself perishes.

The substance of God is that limitless sea, and the waves on its surface are the things of this world. People of contemplation see that there are eighteen thousand worlds and that whatever there is in the world exists as form and is only seen in their forms.

There are hundreds of wonderful forms on the surface of the earth and each form has many shades of colors. Imagine the environs of the seas or mineral mines, or the deserts, or flower gardens, or the place of larks and nightingales where all kinds of colorful flowers and tulips can destroy them. Or envision the many climates, countries, rivers, springs and mountains

with the green grass and air that surround them. Perhaps there are many more things yet than the grass and air.

Around them is the nine layered sky, the constant planets and groups of glorious angels. They are limitless and many in quantity. The invisible uncharted stars looked like the earth's body in it. Four elements, seven heavens and six sides comprise the unique basis of the universe. The greatest creation of the universe is humanity. Their perfection is unperceivable.

Whatever you consider humanity to be: common people or belonging to a high class, sultans with power, or lords, or philosophers and scholars who change religious rules and would establish new sects, divided tribes, or united communities let them all belong. And imagine saints who are considered wise among the people, to be messengers sent from God, see all of them as the waves of God's sea and each wave to be a human being. However, all are temporary. They have fleeting qualities and eternity is not part of their makeup.

The tossing of the sea creates various waves and patterns that disperse in all directions. If the sea is not vexed then you will see no sign of waves.

Anyone who is wise should know that from the beginning till eternity everything that exists in this world has a form but not existence. Everything except the almighty God is nothing and temporary. Only he alone is everlasting. He fastened the order of existence and its representative is accepted without refusal. Everybody, even a person who has drunk life-giving water, will pass away in this world. If you want to be forever, you need to make yourself nothing.

CXLIX

A Story

Shaikh Abul Abbos,[85] belonged to the butchers. He was a powerful mullah. He stepped into the Valley of Nothingness and lost his essence there.

One day he was sitting in the large room of the mosque and around him were gathered his companions. Suddenly, a strange ascetic came into the

---

[85] Abbul Abbos Qassob Omuliy was a famous Shaikh. His real name was Ahmad bin Muhammad bin Abdulkarim. He died in 921.

room without permission and went straight to the pulpit and said,

'O inhabitants of this room! Listen attentively to my words! Get a jug full of water for me! I would like to purify myself and do my ablutions.'

When the honorable shah heard it, he ordered a jug to be brought out to him. A dervish who lived there brought him a beautiful jug full of water. That lowly man broke the jug and asked for another. The dervish brought another and immediately the man broke it as well. When the dervish informed the Shaikh, he told the dervish to keep bringing the man jugs no matter how many he broke.

The man broke as many jugs as was brought to him, one by one with a stone. Finally the attendants begged his pardon and told him all the jugs they had were broken and no other jug was left in the mosque.

Then he said:

'If you do not have anything else, go back and tell your Shaikh to bring his long beard here, and let him fulfill my obligation!'

When the Shaikh heard these immodest words he jumped to his feet and went in the man's direction. He said: 'Oh, what a happy time! Look, I am the son of a butcher's and I have a beard that I have washed, combed, and taken care of for years and now the time has come for it to be of use. A dervish wants to do a favor and be free of his grief.'

The Shaikh had a glorious white beard. Holding his beard he went to that man.

He was an ignorant, thoughtless, and perhaps, senseless man. When he saw the quality of the Shaikh's nothingness, he did not find any strength for foolish raving. He put his head on the ground below the Shaikh's feet and lost consciousness.

The master who had achieved nothingness looked at him and not a trace of self remained. He made the one who had lost his way perfect and turned copper into gold. Everybody should get rid of his or her color, decoration and paint; otherwise to do this kind of work is not possible.

"Oh Foni, ask God for inexistence like this as well! To obtain such inexistence, is to obtain eternal existence!"

CL

Khoja Bahovuddin Naqshband's Words on How to Obtain Perfect Nothingness

The owner of the highest qualities, the honorable Khoja Bahovuddin Naqshband was the shah of God's virtue and flower seller of the right way. When he was on the throne of this country, he became the king of inexistence. When traveling pure this Truth Knower would compare his essence with various things. However, he considered himself to be less than all of them, and treated himself poorly like a flower before a cypress.

One day he saw a scabrous dog that was far from being clean. The Shaikh compared it with himself and while the tears flowed he began sighing. He said:

'This dog belongs to the faithful but I do not. I cannot say that I am equal to him. He does not know anything other than loyalty to God, but as for me I anguish God!'

When the watchful Shaikh said this the dog passed by him. When the Shaikh saw the traces left by the dog on the ground, he continued comparing and said:

'Am I this trace or more?'

And he said to himself:

'O shameless person! These traces are a sign from the feet of the faithful, while I drag my feet towards disloyalty.'

When he finished speaking, he kissed the ground, and began rubbing the dog's footmarks on his face.

People of God deny their essence and get rid of their existence like this. When no mark remains of self, they sip from the goblet of nothingness. Not finding eternity in God's essence and not being able to see his face in the goblet of oneness, they then join the people of inexistence and reach absolute existence.

CLI

A Group of Moths Discuss the True Candle

One night several moths gathered and tried to get to a candle. They got their wings ready to burn in the fire. 'We are searchers, searching for a

sign in the light of the candle. Whatever we find there we should explain. Let us make known where we come from.'

After this, one of the moths flew to the candle to know its truth. He saw a group of moths high above that gathered in the dark night and there was a candle burning in the center. The moth's eyes were full of the candle's glow and burning there he explained the candle to everybody. However, some did not comprehend it and as for the rest of the moths it did not reach their hearts. No matter how clearly a moth tried to explain the listeners saw no sense in it. When the words of the first moth were no good, the next moth would fly to the candle. It entered the feast of the candle and looked at its glow attentively. Like the former moth he burned and no matter how much he spoke the moths did not understand his what he was getting at. Then another moth tried it and flew around the head of the candle many times. He also did not obtain the goal and solve the problem.

The others were also distressed and tried to reach the goal by being swift. They kept flying around the candle and each burnt their wings and tails. As much as they burned their goal was attained, however, it was difficult to explain it, and considered forbidden to narrate. For a person cannot explain the ray with the tongue. If one does not burn he will not be able to know its content.

When a moth found out the truth nothing remained since his body became ash. He was not afraid when he threw himself into the flame. The body parts that burned became pure and turned into flame. For what he wanted he realized. Within his goal he perished and attained the very thing needed for inexistence. He found out the truth and this was enough with no words of explanation needed.

If people pay attention to these moths they will have two viewpoints. First, it is impossible to solve the problem without burning and to attain the goal without unity with the candle. Not until he puts himself in the flame of the candle what he has and does not have will not burn and if he does not enter into the flame of his goal, his desired lover will not show her face.

Second, when lightning like this makes its fire sink into the sea, there is no chance to say a word about it, and it is impossible explain anything about the secret of this work. Anyone who does not burn cannot solve it for anyone else and whoever does burn the others will not know what happened to him.

"O Foni! Stop going on about inexistence! To attain union is good.

Burn in the fire of nothingness! Like a moth flying around the candle's flame, throw yourself into the light. You will be in the goal you desire when nothing remains of your essence and body but your goal! If people don't know of this event, let them remain unaware."

CLII

What Shaikh Sufyon Savri said about Achieving Eternity from Nothingness

Shaikh Sufyon Savri[86] was a leader of people who knew much about religion. May Allah make his place be full of light forever! Once when he was speaking about enlightenment one of his students asked him:

'If anyone wants to see God, how can he do it?'

The Shaikh answered:

'You should know that the journey consists of one thousand destinations and each of them has maladies and disasters. Between the fire and rays are found seven seas and their width is limitless. If you want to cross these seas a huge fish with his trap will appear in front of you. He is such a terrible fish that in one breath he can completely swallow up all the living things of two worlds. His home is the sea of need and he swims all around it.'

CLIII

The Birds Find A Sign of Eternity at the End of the Valley of Nothingness

Finally, the face of the words became thoroughly veiled and questions and answers came to an end. It cannot really be explained how difficult it now was for these birds who had been listening to these words. They realized that this work was extremely difficult to fulfill and that the group would not be able to do it. Therefore, they gave up hoping and were left with unending sorrow. When they heard similar tragic words from Hoopoe, all of them began to raise their voices. They now knew the secret of the work and were panic stricken. The panic killed several of them at once,

---

[86] Shaikh Sufyon Savri was a famous Shaikh. His real name was Abul Abdulla Said. He died in 783.

while remaining birds went into shock. They flew for years not knowing rest and were not afraid of the disasters that they encountered. Over the years they traveled the hard and easy routes and they became separated from themselves. They faced so many difficulties that it is impossible to describe them even with one hundred thousand languages. If this road is before you and you traverse it then you will be able to know its hardship. You will realize what they had to endure.

In the long run, with many fractures and wounds, only a minority from this troubled flock were able to attain the goal. For the road was unendingly long, and there were many disasters, pain, and troubles. Therefore, some birds surrendered to the road, some faced severe illness and half got lost on the way. Hardship's bitter wind blew against them and snipped the thread of their lives. On the road there were countless evils and crises and as expected many perished.

As a result, out of the one hundred thousand birds only thirty birds survived the one hundred thousands of difficulties and reached the final place. They were so exhausted that there was no sign of life left in their bodies. Not one wing remained unharmed and their feathers were disheveled like wood shavings. Their body had become weak with road's hardships and their soul writhed with pain and suffering.

When they reached their destination they saw a grand place. It was impossible to measure its width. The whole sky was smaller than a plain straw. From the clouds of needlessness it poured; the thunderstorm rumbled frightfully and the lightening was constant. It was as if a storm of evil rained all over the world and disaster's lightning was burning the whole sky. Seven heavens seemed to be a handful of ground and cedars and trees of paradise seemed to be like worthless straw.

All the birds were surprised and deplored their feebleness. They saw that one hundred bright suns were not even worth one hundredth of a particle here. Their wings and tails caught on fire from it and they began to wail with unending remorse.

'We thirty stupid birds concerned ourselves with what is not to be done. The terror of death was always near and to traverse this road we experienced a lot of difficulties. Did we attain the goal and pass away our life on it? This place is so huge and frightening that we have neither

---

Abdulkarim. He died in 921.

quantity nor quality here!'

When they said this, smoke began to come from their heads. At every moment the wandering birds bumped into hopelessness and it worsened their souls. In short, when the troubled birds could not find the remedy for their sorrows and when they did not have strength to fly and when they did not have the patience to land because of pain, all of a sudden an envoy of honor like a state bird came to them from behind the curtains. When this bird saw the flock tied up in a hundred threads of evil and weak with shock, he desired to ask them about their state:

'Eh, what kind of community is this flock? Who are those who faced thousands of evils but could not find use in it? Who are these losers and wanderers, whose value is equal with dirt? Who are those who were condemned to insult and did not see any purpose in it?'

The birds answered:

'We have been degraded, busy with vain work, and neglected. We left hoping to find a shah and faced a lot of hardship. We had been hoping to get to his home by much suffering. We were an army without a shah. What kind of army has no shah? So many thousands of flocks died from the hardship of the road that it is impossible to count them. Only we thirty have reached this place. We want Semurgh to be our shah and take care of us. If the shah accepts our invitation, we will agree to be his slaves with pleasure!'

Then the envoy said:

'O strayed flock! You unknowingly became a friend to senselessness. You are confused and thinking of unrealizable plans. In this state, with which of your languages will you dare to utter the shah's name? Why did this idea come to your mind?

'You are worth nothing and there is no group as low as you. As for the shah he is above your odd pleasantries. There is no reason to be troubled by you. As if you have an idea of your existence! Actually you have neither number, nor total, nor existence! Your claim that you exist is empty. Your heart is full of unrealistic dreams that will not work.

'It is such a large place that one hundred thousand suns will not be able to shine like one small atom. One hundred thousand raging elephants are like a dead fly! Neither are you there or not there. Your existence and inexistence is minute.

'Don't speak senseless words. Go back where you came from as soon as possible. If you have anything else to say, tell it as you leave!'

When the birds heard it, they became baffled and weak, and lost consciousness. They sought asylum in each other but began to burn in the fire of hopelessness. They said to themselves:

'Oh no! It is a pity that all our efforts were in vain! It is a pity we endured such assaults!

'If a shah has so high place here how can we present ourselves to him? Will he not have time for feeble us? Everything we did in hope is gone! All our dreams to reach the eternal state were in vain!'

All the birds were stricken with depression, unending sorrow and unfulfilled desire. They exclaimed:

'Have you ever seen a pitiful flock like us that was so far from their dream and hope?'

CLIV

When the Birds Were Hopeless in Achieving Nothingness Hoopoe Showed Them the Right Way and Their Strength was Restored

Hoopoe said to them:

'O poor flock whose household is troubled! Do not be hopeless of the shah's compassion, for one of his qualities is to show mercy. If it is difficult to reach him it is also a good thing to die of his love.

'We have obtained this happy fate and today reached his home. This joy itself is our high place. And now it is alright for us to die.'

Hearing these words all the birds expressed to Hoopoe that they did not need this:

'O wise speaker! We accepted all your orders and endured all the evil that came before us. Wherever you flew we did not separate ourselves from you. Whatever you ordered we did not refuse. However, when it was time to be happy seeing him we met separation's sorrow. What you said did not come out right!'

Hoopoe said to them:

'Do not fall into depression or be abused by it at all. Our aim was to see the shah and reach his place. When we started we were ready to face the hardship. Do not doubt that you are far from your original goal as we have now found the driveway to his house.

'If the lover reaches true perfection in his love, then both separation and union will be considered equal by him. For what the sweetheart wishes is a dream for her lover. Whatever she wants will be considered acceptable. If you cannot be united with the sweetheart, isn't it enough for you to live with her memory? If any lover dies with the memory of his sweetheart than his death will be equal to an eternal life.'

CLV

A Story

A man met Majnun in the wasteland. Majnun was talking to himself, and so the man asked him:

'Whom are you speaking to?'

'O happy man, I am speaking to Laili', answered Majnun.

'She is far from you, isn't she?' said the man.

'O ignorant one, she has taken the place of my heart! Since my heart is fed by the memory of her and the road is so far how can I forget her?'

"Whoever reaches perfection in love his existence will be formed by the memory of his beloved. If you want to speak much of love you must accept it when sadness comes to you instead of happiness."

CLVI

The Birds Reach Great Nothingness and Eternal Union

These travelers crossed many seas and lands and reached their desired place. They were not tired of traveling night and day no matter what troubles came. When they obtained their wishes a curtain was closed and the flock could not see the beauty. The confounded birds did not give up what they believed even though he displayed his greatness and resisted them. Although some of them were irritated, Hoopoe kept them from the road of discouragement and bitterness by his words and sermons.

They came alive from what Hoopoe said and their difficulties became easy once again. For they had become friends of loyalty and devotion, and in searching for the beloved the use of these two attitudes goes far. If they became lowly and weak before greatness, Hoopoe urged them not to fret and provided many examples. They had courage and their perfect

leader was wise.

Therefore, their loyalty and devotion brought them to the second nothingness,[87] This is the highest state of nothingness. In Sufism it means to reach God spiritually. and the beloved became their companion. There, the wind of compassion blew from the garden of union; Christ's pure breath came and took away the curtains that veiled them one by one. These curtains containing rays and darkness were taken aside. The flower of destination and happiness blossomed in the garden of union and the sweet scent of their neck pleased the heart. The brokenness of the birds' hearts disappeared as they obtained their goal of union and happiness.

Every flower in this garden was like a mirror. Wherever they looked they saw themselves. Besides this, there were rays, purity, clearness and hidden things there. It was like looking in a mirror or in clear water. Everything could be seen from head to foot, and it resembled a person seeing his reflection in a mirror or still water.

The goal of the thirty birds was to arrive here enduring a lot of hardship and see Semurgh's own face and achieve eternal life through nothingness. However, wherever they looked they saw themselves. Allah! Allah! What a beautiful word that the thirty birds that dreamed to see Semurgh see themselves as Semurgh![88] As if a precious stone was turned into a pearl, the secret of 'min araf'[89] became revealed.

"Oh heart! These words with their delicate meaning are the language of the birds and it is the language of the people who are aware of its value. Although these words meaning is difficult and broad, with pain it will become clear. For pain in humanity eradicates the wild beast. If a person is able to deny their ego in this way nothing will stay except spiritual purity. Do not try to argue with this!

"Humanity embodies such glory that if one gets rid of their bad morals and does not imitate Pharaoh one will have nothing but good qualities like Moses. Or if he looses the qualities of Abu Jahl that he has, like Habibulloh he will have high glory and be aware of existence and inexistence. He will climb the staircase of unity and know purity's secrets. His eyes will

---

[87] This is the highest state of nothingness in Sufism. It means to reach God spiritually.

[88] See footnote four above.

[89] The Hadith starts with these words. It says: 'he who knows himself he knows, he knows his owner (God).'

be bright from the ray of union and the notions of "my" and "yours" will disappear between them.

"God's essence creates the sea's waves. What damage can the waves do to the sea? The sea is considered to be a sea whether its water has waves or not, but there is no wave without water. The existence of the wave depends on the sea.

"If you mediate on this or love's secrets you will be mingling with God's qualities and with your awareness you will dare to say that the main aim of creation is you! There is nothing but you! You are a perfect description and one who understands the difficulties of existence! That is why you ponder your existence and whatever you want you search for in yourself!

"You are an amazing attractive bird in the garden of Paradise and you are pure in the flower garden of glory. However, the flock that sought Semurgh found the way traveling under hardship. They were devoted to this road and from this seeking union resulted. You also have a chance. If you fix your bad qualities, you will attain the goal! If you are not devoted to this way, and speak lowly or embellished words, you are sure to be hung.

"Whoever understands the meaning should know that, the tongue is too short to utter these words. For each word and its meaning is different. The one who is occupied with words will not understand its meaning.

"What meaning I knew I tried to explain in the language of the birds. What I said should not be understood by its external meaning, do not let the faces of deep meanings be shrouded. My words are only understandable to those who know the language of the birds. As soon as they perceive the meaning they will start to panic.

"However, a shrewd bird will understand what its implications are at once. These words are the most difficult of words; it is the language of the person with no language. The requirement is that the person who understands it should not feel free to explain it as disaster may come upon his tongue.

"O God! I repent of the words I have uttered. I seek your shelter for my forbidden words. I did not intend to outline these thoughts on my own. Perhaps, I gave a commentary on Attar's words. Save my words from disaster. Remember that you know whom I am following. If I made a mistake then it is just a shortcoming, because many letters were written on the pages of perfection. If I misused words, then consider them to be because of my perfect guide. I followed him and spoke about you. Accept my pardon and forgive my sins."

CLVII

An Example to Ponder of One's Excuse for His Defect

There lived an absent-minded ascetic. He became needy because of someone else. The one he fell in love with was the most beautiful woman and her coquetry was deadly for the people. She was so beautiful that even the beauties of Paradise and fairies were no match to her, and the moon and the sun did not look beautiful before her.

The world was caught in the clamor of her beauty as the commotion spread to many cities and countries. Although her beauty was so indescribable she was famous along with two other people. The first one was a master of knowledge and astuteness; the second one was a master of making people feel grief.

One day the ascetic who was in love remembered his sweetheart and compared her face with a flower, her figure with a cypress, her look with a peacock, her walking with a pheasant. When he was articulating these words that pleased him the moon-like darling came near him and listened to what he said from a hidden place.

After a brief while she walked up to him and said:

'Your descriptions of me are nothing but sarcasm. I am extremely ashamed of them. You said that my figure looked like a cypress, but can a cypress walk gracefully like me? You said my face looked like a flower, but which flower has eyes and eyebrows that kill? You compared my look with a peacock, but when does a peacock make people senseless and unconscious? You compared my walking with a pheasant, but what pheasant has been the cause of people's death?'

The moon-like faced girl continued to shout at him in rage. The lover did not know how to properly respond to her:

'I have made a mistake, and I am extremely ashamed of it, nevertheless, I am the one who describes you and I am a sinful slave!'

When she heard it she retorted at once:

'I will destroy your existence from the world!'

He dropped himself to the ground and implored:

'O one who made the women of Paradise and fairies humble of their beauty! Everything that I said about you is because of my love for you, my devotion for you, and my friendship for you. They do not contain a trace of complaint, scorn or sarcasm.

'However, when I was praising you there was defect in my description. I admit that. Now if you do not want to have compassion I am ruined. If you consider what I said to be ignorance and all of it crude then the shame will kill me senseless. If you want to kill me then it would be very hard for me!'

When the ascetic accepted his shortcoming and begged for pardon, the beauty was gracious and forgave him.

One of the leaders of this road Abdulla Ansoriy has said the following:

'O one who has pure faith, you should know that a person who arranges the tune of a composition and sings a song and the goal of this tune and song is to remember God. This work is better than to recite the lines of the Qur'an using tunes of ignorance.

'If the tune and song contain awareness it is be better than wandering during the time of prayer.'

CLVIII

Begging Forgiveness for Mistakes and Sins

"O ruler of all people and generous invisible God! The reason generous people exist is you. There are no bounds to your grace and goodness, and your generosity and gifts are innumerable. I beg your forgiveness for whatever I have written to describe you, however inappropriate it was. Not only me but also many great scholars have written about you over the years. They also will have to recognize that they were blind.

"If a perplexed Foni like me has said anything about your truth, pardon his errors and short-comings because of grace and forgive the good and bad writings. Whatever I did with my pencil, it was of you I wrote. I did not think of anybody else but you and this is enough for me. More or less what I told was of you. Truth or lie it also was of you. No matter how aware I was of your secrets I described them with the language of the birds.

"This time I implore you with the language of the birds, as I am lost like a half slaughtered bird. For not every bird is able to speak sweetly, use fine meaning, and be fluent. If a nightingale graciously recites to you

wonderful epic poems,[90] the crow will not stop his obnoxious tunes. So, not every bird's singing will be soothing, nor every bird's song irritating.

"I spoke on their behalf, but of course not every bird's singing has one rhythm. Although a parrot and mina can speak like a man, each one has its own speech. There is a difference in their singing. One speaks of God and another about an idol. While one has disbelief, the second one has religion.

"However, Foni's work is not with blasphemy or religion. For whatever he has said he said because of you! Cover over his errors with a curtain so that at the feast of nothingness he may take a sip of wine. O Lord, when it is time for his goblet of nothingness, do not forget to make it eternal."

---

[90] 'Dastans.'

Printed in the United States
70052LV00002B/202-285

9 781425 912482